TRYSTING

TRYSTING

Emmanuelle Pagano

Translated by Jennifer Higgins & Sophie Lewis

Two Lines Press

Originally published as: *Nouons-nous* by Emmanuelle Pagano
© 2013 by P.O.L éditeur

Translation © 2016 by Jennifer Higgins and Sophie Lewis
Published by arrangement with And Other Stories Publishing, UK

Two Lines Press
582 Market Street, Suite 700, San Francisco, CA 94104
www.twolinespress.com

ISBN 978-1-931883-56-6

Library of Congress Control Number: 2016938373

Cover design by Gabriele Wilson
Cover photo by Chloe Edwards/Millennium Images, UK
Typeset by Jessica Sevey

Printed in the United States of America

1 3 5 7 9 10 8 6 4 2

This project is supported in part by an award from
the National Endowment for the Arts.

ART WORKS.
arts.gov

I wake up, and I can hear the sound of little creatures walking around on an invisible piece of cloth stretched tight next to my ear, stretched between me and him. Between me and him, just enough room for a cloth pulled taut like paper. I open my eyes and it's nearly light. He's scratching his stubble. The tiny sounds stop as he smiles at me. His hand leaves his cheek to touch mine.

✳

It's been a long time without her now. I'm starting to get used to the loneliness, the evenings, the little seven o'clock sadness.

✳

My parents had an orchard, their pride and joy, which took up all their spare time. They would be there before work in the morning, as soon as they got home at night, and often even after dinner. We took advantage of this to meet in secret, in my bedroom. I could see the orchard from my window, and kept an eye on my parents' movements between lingering kisses. The trees were perfectly aligned, almost to the centimeter. Each bore its allotted fruit and stood in regimented order with no room for confusion: cherries, apples, apricots, and then in front of them pears, figs, and plums; then, in front of them again, close to my window, came rows of bushes supported by stakes and metal wire. The scent of thousands of raspberries, blueberries, and red currants perfumed my long lie-ins when, at my mother's daily insistence, I opened the window to air the room. I used to laugh at my parents and their steely rigor. It wouldn't have surprised me if they had decided to plant the whole orchard in alphabetical order. But once, while we were making fun of them, complicit in an over-long embrace, my father burst in, chased him away, and punished me for my disobedience. Confined to my bedroom in the middle of August, pensive at my window, I daydreamed and looked out at the orchard. I hoped that he would come and rescue me. He came the next night. I heard the sound of branches moving. It was very hot, so I had an excuse for leaving the window open. I could see him darting around among the trees, stripped to the waist, up to something. He wasn't alone. From far away, he blew me a kiss, signaling that I should go back to sleep. I got back into bed, disappointed. At first light, I rushed to the window. My father was already in the orchard, frozen before the spectacle of metamorphosis, his transformed fruit trees. The peach trees were hung with pears, the pear trees were heavy with apricots, the apricots had been replaced by plums, and from the plum trees swung fresh figs. He had spent the night working on this little act of revenge with the help of his many friends. They had picked every single fruit and, carefully attaching a loop of fishing line to each stalk, had swapped them all around.

✸

She releases me from ordinary life in a perfectly ordinary way, just by the way she moves, by the way she moves and speaks. She has a different way of being.

✸

My partner is an accordionist. He plays for dances, weddings, birthdays, and retirement parties, or sometimes he does the musical interludes at cultural events, readings, poetry, talks on local history, that sort of thing. I met him at my best friend's wedding. I was bored and trying to amuse myself by watching the other guests. I always have a book in my bag but I was afraid of seeming rude if I got it out. So I watched people. They all looked tense and ill at ease. Only one person was opening his arms wide, and it was him. To make his music, he was embracing the air, welcoming the empty space, breathing with easy movements. I fell into the circle of his arms. Quite literally, I found myself filling that hollow, those great bellows, his musical chest. I wanted to hear the sounds of his big heart, disrupted by desire and then set right by the accordion.

＊

Because I had injured my hands and they were in bandages for several days, he washed and tended me down to the details, down to the navel, to folds of skin, down to cotton buds, to the combing caress of an eyebrow.

＊

Loving him means worrying about him. The air solidifies in my throat. My stomach is full of heavy objects. I try to find things for my body to do. Walking, cooking, washing clothes, cleaning the floors. I try to think about mundane things, to crowd out this anxiety that's so full, full of him, to replace it with light and inoffensive preoccupations. But the worry takes me by the throat, or by the stomach, as soon as I stop. Then my body reminds me of the weight in my stomach, in my throat, this weight of loving him.

*

The police said that it was probably a voluntary disappearance. I spent months searching for her, months that stretched into years in the end. Then I decided to stop, and began to go out and meet people again. One evening, I got home a little earlier than usual and put the television on. I ended up half-asleep in front of a documentary on alternative lifestyles—people living in yurts, teepees, tree houses, pods, all that grassroots eco-warrior crap. I had almost dropped off when I saw her. She was coming out of a hut, all grubby and utterly beautiful.

*

He rang my doorbell. He was selling calendars. Over coffee, he explained that he'd bought them up front, but that, of course, he recovered from sales the twenty-five years he had already advanced. I laughed at his slip of the tongue. It was true, though. He was selling time and I wasn't getting any younger.

*

He doesn't like eating anything that still has its skin on. He thrusts it aside with his tongue or his fingers before carrying the flesh to his mouth. He unrolls the blood sausage from its casing, holding the skin down carefully with his fork. Even grapes and figs have to be peeled. I make fun of his fussiness. But I let him get on with it, and my teasing is gentle and affectionate. Sometimes I extract the pulp for him and put it into a little dish, then rinse my fingers.

*

His son had a birthday party this afternoon, and my son was invited. When we arrived, he was blowing up balloons. He made me a coffee as I stood with a few other parents who were still hanging around, and then he sent us all away, telling us to come back and collect our children around five or six o'clock. Yes, he'd cope fine by himself. My son fell asleep in the car on the way home, tired out from the games and full of sweets, the balloons he had brought back as souvenirs floating around him. I didn't wake him up right away when we got back. I caught hold of a big, bright yellow balloon, pressed the opening to my lips, and let it deflate slowly, breathing in his air.

*

She and I have been playing a waiting game right from the start. I'm always the one waiting and she's always late. I've gotten used to it. I arrive on time because I never know exactly how late she's going to be. Sometimes just a few minutes, sometimes more, much much more. I arrive at our meeting place and say to myself: Here goes. I read. I always bring a book with me but after a couple of chapters I'm already worrying, despite myself. I carry on worrying for who knows how many pages.

✴

He had begun his adult life by dying, as many adolescents do, but unlike most, he never stopped doing it. He would die regularly, every two or three years or so, and nobody could say or do anything to stop him. After each failed attempt, he would bounce back, rediscover his enthusiasm for life, and meet a new woman. Sometimes it was actually the same woman but they always seemed new to him. As far as he was concerned, it was a complete regeneration each time. With each new life, he was unashamedly joyful. I was one of those new women: the last. During his revivals, he even had children, one with me. He was alive. And then, without showing any signs of it at first, he would die. His four children were thriving, they loved him, I loved him, he had a good job, everything was fine, and suddenly, just like that, he was dying again. Only to be reborn. As new. You might almost think that he had simply metamorphosed, shed his skin, if it weren't for all the scars, the traces of his deaths, which were deeper and more numerous each time. He had never taken pills; his deaths were always violent. He'd die by hanging, drowning, or shooting. The second-to-last time took off the bottom half of his face, but he still got up smiling, smiling without a chin.

✳

When he was in my apartment, he would constantly bang into things. He couldn't find the doors or the switches and he kept forgetting where the furniture was. Every protruding chair leg was a potential trap. When he was in my apartment he was clumsy and blind, as though he wasn't really there.

✳

I live in this city, this crowded, expensive city hemmed in by freeways. We're very cramped here, living, eating, and sleeping all packed together. Space is an arrogant luxury, and when you look up, the skies are always at once oversized and out of reach. I walk along the streets with my head thrown back, dreaming of height and air. In the apartment, I can't stretch my arms out fully without touching shelves, furniture, a wall, a door, objects, my partner. We pile up our things as best we can, and when we can pile no more, we resign ourselves to the job of sorting. We try to decide how important the things we own actually are, according to our own odd set of criteria. We weigh the bulk of the thing against the memories it contains, the encumbrance versus the attachment. Then we consider the correlations of our lives. This causes arguments. Calibrating two sets of memories, affections, and idiosyncrasies is a delicate business. We attach different significance to things and emotions. Until now, he and I only ever had minor clashes, always staying on the right side of friendly. Little skirmishes about nothing, never any hostile arguments. But this business of sorting, after a decade or so of shared lives, of tenderness, and of more and more stuff, mine, his, ours, threatens our little shared corner of space and time. We begin to get in one another's way. Now I spend my evenings out in the streets, walking around with my head down. On one of these dawdling walks, as I am putting off the moment when I have to go home, I come up with a simple solution that has never occurred to us before. Storage units.

They're underground spaces, like huge rigid cardboard boxes in ultramodern cellars that you can walk or even drive into. You go into a sort of garage, but it's less like a garage than a tiny city-within-a-city, with its own traffic, roads, and alleyways between the units. At the entrance to this miniature city, a very helpful attendant explains how it works. He shows me around and unlocks one of the empty units so that I can see inside. It's very clean and well lit, and I'm sure that my partner will feel as relieved as I do. I ask myself why we thought of it so late, so late in our life together, so late in our relationship, our dusty bric-a-brac. We sign the lease with the excitement of young newlyweds. But before we can move, we need to sort, to decide which things will be taken away, stored, kept at a distance, temporarily expelled from our apartment. It is only then that I realize that all we've done is move the problem. We still have to sort, assess, and calculate how many square meters we have. Our dithering becomes disproportionate, and we've reached the point of considering separate apartments when one night I shut myself in the storage unit and have a good, proper cry, screaming and howling as our city never lets us do.

＊

Everybody is looking at us. He gets embarrassed and tries to stifle my laughter with his hand, which molds to my mouth. I carry on laughing into his fingers and he starts laughing too because it tickles.

＊

She doesn't want to talk to me in front of her son. She doesn't want to break it off with me in front of him. She doesn't want to say it—I'm leaving you—in front of him. He and I have gotten along well all these years. I drop him off at school, collect him in the afternoon, make him snacks, and help him with his homework. We go for walks together, or to the movie theater or the park. She doesn't come because she's always at work. When she does finally come home she wants to talk to me, keeps saying that she wants to talk to me, one-on-one. I know what she has to say to me one-on-one. I don't want to hear it. I stick to her son for as long as I can, as often as I can. I don't let him out of my sight. She'll never have the chance to talk to me alone.

❋

He puts his arms around me and then draws back a little. He pulls my T-shirt away at the neck and looks over my shoulder at my back. I can tell he's looking at something by the way he stops moving. He isn't stroking me or kissing me or doing anything, just holding the neck of my T-shirt. I say What is it? He says: you.

❋

After I've visited the chapel, the attendant asks me to join him for a drink, and I do. At the café he puts his key down on the table. It's a big, heavy key with a rounded end. He starts to talk about his work and takes the big key in his hand, weighing it in his palm as he tells me that this is only a copy, this one, that the original was more impressive still. It was fifty centimeters long—can you imagine? And at the other end there was another key, a smaller one, so it was two keys in one, one at each end, a double key, and you could use one end to open the little cloister window, you see, to get a look at whoever was wanting to come in, and the other end to open the door: one key to have a look, one key to open up. He repeats this key story quite a few times and then says that I can touch it, even take it in my hand if I want to. He's a bore, just like his key.

✳

When he's asleep his usual face disappears and his features relax. He looks like a man at peace. Beside me in the bed, there's somebody different.

✳

I was kneeling on the ground making bundles of wood. He was shouting. I started to cry as I arranged the branches according to size and tied them together with rough string. I took off one of my leather gloves so that I could wipe away my tears and continued my work, forgetting to put it back on. When he stopped shouting, I noticed that I had cut myself with the string.

✳

I never used to feel at home in her apartment because it was so dirty. I'm very particular, and I don't like there to be even a speck of dust around the house. She never washed her clothes, just kept wearing the same old things. She didn't have a washing machine and seemed to know nothing of laundromats. She never washed the floor or the bathroom or the toilet. Just sometimes she would sweep the kitchen, leaving the pile of dust pushed into a corner. I used to wait until she was out and then do a bit of cleaning, because she got angry if I did so much as look at a sponge in her presence. I brought my vacuum cleaner over in secret. After a few weeks the apartment had started to look very different and she noticed. She threw me out, along with all the cleaning products I had hidden behind the trashcan under the sink.

✳

The more he reads me, the less he loves me.

✳

She leans to the right whenever she's standing still. It isn't that one of her legs is shorter than the other, it's just something she does naturally to ease her nagging sciatica. She drops all the weight of her body on the right side so the left goes up, as if her hips were an old-fashioned balance, a pan scale. I watch her as she goes toward the sink to do the dishes. She's talking to me, not thinking about what she's doing. She puts some dish soap on the sponge and gets to work; the scales tip. I walk over and, standing behind her, take her in my arms. Her body regains its equilibrium, supported by mine.

※

I was so happy to have her near me that I fell asleep for two days.

※

Somebody took my hand when I arrived in intensive care. It must have been a nurse. I couldn't see her because my face was swollen and bleeding and my eyelids were puffed up. I couldn't open my eyes without crying out in pain. The hand that took mine was so soft it had to be a woman's, so young-feeling, and so very soft and warm. A stranger's hand. I kept asking them to call her, to let her know. The young woman's hand wasn't helping me or calming me down. I could barely speak, I couldn't hear anything at all, and between bouts of vomiting I kept asking them, through my hiccups and my tears, to just call her. The hand held mine without hurting me and without comforting me. And suddenly that hand drew away and was replaced by a different one. This hand was rough and wrinkled. I squeezed it hard. It was old, twisted by years of work, by life, all this life of ours.

＊

He was crying, down below my stomach, over my labia, and I didn't know how to comfort him. I grasped his shoulders to try to pull him up toward my face. I would have liked to say something to him but he wouldn't move. He stayed there, forehead pressed to my thighs, eyelashes brushing against my pubic hair just where the flesh parts. Tears trickled inside, all warm.

＊

He changes into his swimming trunks, spreads out his towel, and lies down. I'm hesitant about getting undressed. It's very hot but there's something holding me back. I unfold my towel too, but feel awkward, as though I'm taking up too much space. The beach is a narrow strip of suffocating shade at the bottom of a high cliff which keeps on shedding stones. On the clifftop the sun is still perilously hot although it's late in the afternoon, and adventurous buzzards are circling in its punishing light. They seem to taunt the seagulls flying below them on graceful wings. Just you try to fly this high. The sea crashes very close to us, foaming but heavy at the same time. It's too violent for me, much too rough for me to swim. I try to read but can't concentrate. I don't trust these surroundings and I don't feel safe. I look at him, and that reassures me. He smiles. I know he thinks I'm silly to be afraid of the stones. He says Don't worry, there won't be an avalanche. He seems so calm. I could go anywhere with him, even here.

✳

When he plays I don't hear the music, I hear his hands. I hear the sound of his fingers as they move and press on the neck of the guitar, the tiny, precise taps of hard nails on strings. I hear the squeak as he shifts the bar formed by the tensed joints of his index finger, a wrenching sound that the melody can never entirely hide.

✳

Anything I didn't give him, I didn't keep. Anything I didn't give him is lost.

✳

I'd never managed to lose weight. I'd been really fat ever since I was very little, I'd been fat forever. I'd tried everything: diets, pills, cleanses, but I was a hopeless case. Then, a few months ago, she left me. True, she didn't leave me because of my weight, but all of a sudden that weight seemed like a heavier burden to carry, more unbearable than ever. I couldn't stand myself anymore. I hadn't been there for her, or at least not enough. I wanted to become a different person and love her in the way I should always have loved her. I was hoping to win her back. I hated myself and I needed to change, be less selfish, get rid of a part of me. I had a lot of ego to lose. Dozens of kilos too much of me. Losing weight was easy but required patience. It took a year, but I wanted to take my time, face up to myself. I lost fifty kilos. I made a special wooden box and inside it I put ten brass five-kilo weights. I had little messages for her engraved onto each one. I wrapped the box up in special paper, loaded it onto a little cart, and went to present her with my lost weight.

✷

The first thing I noticed about her was the scar right in the middle of her face. Even people who seem to know her well often say she doesn't have one. But she does. It's a lovely invisible welt that only shows when she feels moved. I didn't know it then, but what I was seeing in the sudden reddening of the mark was her emotion at seeing me. It appears when her feelings get the better of her, scoring a line through her beautiful face. She says she can feel it burning, from her chin to her forehead. It still glows red, just sometimes, when she looks at me.

✳

I went to the post office to get the letters rerouted. His letters, to my address. As though he had moved in with me. As though he'd finally agreed to my request to live together. As though he hadn't fled in the face of my eagerness. Now I read his mail, including all the letters from his new girlfriend. They're urgent and worried just like mine used to be. And, of course, he never replies.

✳

By now, I've got an idea of what he smells like, and having an idea of somebody's smell means you're ready to start getting used to it.

✳

I don't see the clothes as clothes, but as cloth for her body: cotton, wool, silk, nylon, linen, anything; it's all thigh cloth or knee cloth, wrist, neck, or stomach cloth.

✳

I wear ear protection when I'm working because my job's so noisy. It's the noise of trees and power tools: lots of squealing, tearing, banging, cracking, scraping, and the din of motors. I've got a sturdy body and strong thighs, good for gripping branches. I'm a freelance arborist, otherwise known as a tree surgeon. Depending on what you need, I'm a trimmer, a pruner, and a feller. But I'm not a fella, like most arborists. I'm a woman and I'm an arborist. Not an "arboristess," thankfully: I'm glad it's not a word with "ess" on the end. I'd always rather be someone's master than their mistress—and I do often feel like a master of the forest when I'm at the top of one of these damaged giants. I can see for miles. I feel powerful when I'm on the ground, too, when I climb down and inspect the trees from underneath. I can still see a long way, but now it's through time rather than through space. I observe. I predict. I look at the structure and the foliage and I can read the tree's future. I know whether it needs pruning or felling. Sometimes I climb so high that it's as though I'm perched, alone, transported into the future of mankind and the landscape.

My husband, on the other hand, always keeps his feet firmly on the ground. He doesn't even know the names of the different varieties of tree.

He's never really understood why I do this job. Why I insist on losing myself in the crowns of the trees, outfitted with a mask and earplugs, chopping away amidst a huge racket, and all for peanuts. To be frank the pay is awful. And it was francs in those days, when our relationship was still holding up. These days we argue a lot, and now the bottom line is in euros. Before, he would watch me as I abseiled down the long tree trunks and he liked coming to see me wherever I was working. I think he found me sexy, strapped into the harness with the chainsaw on my back. When I had it in my hands, my thighs gripping a solid bough, and I started up the motor and shouted at him to get out of the way, raising my voice over the rending sound of the doomed limb, he wanted me then. There's none of that anymore, even though I still plunge down through the treetops like a Cartesian diver. But a Cartesian diva? There's no such thing.

He wants me to leave the trees now, and stay at home. I've never seen him split a single log, though, despite those big strong arms that I still nestle in, once in a while, when I leave the arms of the ashes and the beeches.

✳

We had separated. He had said it's over, I'm leaving. We were still living together while he looked for another place. I couldn't bear this cohabitation. I couldn't bear having him so close by but not being able to touch him. When I was in bed in the evening, I would hear him masturbating in the bathroom and, as a sort of desperate, useless revenge, I got into the forlorn habit of masturbating at the same time as him, silent and listening. He never noticed.

✳

She has atmospheric pains: her joints flare up when the pressure drops. Her whole body is racked before a storm, as if struck by warning flashes of lightning. I see her doubled-up with pain and can't do anything to help, except hope that the weather turns fair, sunny, rainy, snowy, whatever, as long as it stays put.

✳

In the middle of this siesta, this high-summer laziness, I feel thirsty but won't get up. He rolls out of bed and leaves the room, and I hear him turning the tap on in the kitchen. He comes back in with his cheeks bulging, his eyes wide with a laugh he can barely hold back. He leans over me and gives me a drink from mouth to mouth and from laugh to laugh.

✳

He was right at the top of turbine number eight, the one that stands a little way off from the others. I'd never actually seen any of the wind-farm maintenance workers before. I often used to walk in the woods nearby and they would drive past me in their shiny black vans with tinted windows. There was something rather mafia-like about these silent, mysterious vehicles, and I did harbor vague suspicions of them, given their invisibility and the huge sums of money at stake. Everybody in the village was falling over themselves to help. When they got stuck in winter, we would rush to get the snowplow from the local garage and clear a path as wide as a highway through the snowdrifts for them. Turbine number eight is in the woods so you don't see it right away, but it makes a worse racket than the storm itself, churning out currents of sound. That day there wasn't a sound to be heard. I was about to skirt around it to get to my path. I looked up, enjoying the silence and pausing for a giddy view of the giant from underneath. The top half of the cabin was open like a screaming mouth, its upper jaw tipped back, and yet soundless, speechless. There was a man inside it, the bottom half of his body pressed against the railings, the top half leaning over, arms stretched out. He was waving to me, signaling from fifty meters above the ground, the mute gestures of his arms multiplied by the enormous, motionless blades around him.

✻

I'm very clumsy. I drop cutlery, smash glasses and plates, and even break my watch when I'm trying to put it on. I cut myself when I'm chopping vegetables. I'm scatterbrained and dreamy, always leaving my body to do its own thing without checking to see what it's up to. When he speaks to me I finally pull myself together. He focuses me.

✳

She wears a bra to bed because she can't bear to feel her breasts lying against her chest, that fold of aging skin that she calls the fold of time. Some nights I lie just behind her, undo her bra, and replace the underwire with my hands. I'm supporting her youth.

✳

He couldn't make love to me, or rather he could, but he did it badly and clumsily, and he never came. He said I can't do it, and it really seemed to hurt him, emotionally as well as physically. He didn't know how to touch me any more than he knew how to let me touch him, and I didn't know what else to try, so I just kept saying it'll happen eventually. That made him angry and he said No, it won't. One evening, when I was taking a bath at his house, he took down a bottle of shampoo from the shelf, an expensive bottle that he'd just bought, specially suited to my hair. I was amazed that he knew which kind was best for me, as we weren't well acquainted yet. He smiled, knelt down next to the bathtub, and washed my hair gently with the shampoo. It was magic shampoo. When I got out of the tub he embraced me with new arms and held me against his transformed body.

✳

I calculate everything. I calculate too much, far too much. I try to work out what he's going to think in advance. I say to myself that if I turn the light off, he'll be annoyed, things like that. I can't behave naturally. I can't seem to love him without making predictions.

✳

I cried over his goodbye letter for days on end with no let-up, no interval, utterly immersed. There was no play-acting. I say that because I'm actually an actor and I know how to cry on demand. My body was shaken, torn with sobs, and this very physical grief wore me out. I trembled all over, my teeth chattered violently, and I couldn't control my body anymore.

Then, dried up, wiped out, and calm, knowing that I had exhausted all my tears and that there was no longer any risk of unseemly paroxysms or wailing, and because it was sunny and I could cover my swollen eyes with sunglasses and not look strange, I went out. When I spoke to people I realized that my voice was completely different. It was all cried out, ruined by the harsh song of my tears, hoarse and muffled, struggling to make itself heard.

✻

I stayed put stubbornly in his arms for ten years, as if between two walls.

✻

I desired him from afar at first, when all I could see was the movement of his body, restricted by the weights he was wearing on his ankles. They were the weights you can buy at sporting goods stores. He was so far away that I could only just see them, but I knew they were there, slowing down his movements. He himself was lighter than air. It wasn't exactly desire I felt when I watched him dance, more an attraction, the attraction between a satellite and a planet, he the satellite, I the planet, though really it was he who attracted me. He attracted me because he was held down, weighted, yet still he danced, danced, danced. In the theater program it said that this dancer was on a quest for his own weight, that he was slowly levitating. His body acted like a balloon. It was this resistance to flight that enchanted me; I found his desire for an anchor touching. As I watched him, I found myself wanting to be that anchor, his. He was facing me now and I was already in love with him. He came closer, dancing, dancing, dancing. And he moved away. He was always pulled away, higher. I wanted to bring him down, back here, so that he could dance, dance, dance. I wanted to take the place of the weights tied with Velcro around his ankles, stoop at his feet, grip him with my fingers, my whole body bending to the task. I would even gain weight if I had to. If he looked as though he were about to fly away I would keep him here among us earthlings. I joined him in his dressing room after the show like a groupie, all ready to get fat. Close up, he was just as insubstantial as from a distance, sitting in his chair and wrestling with his own lightness, trying not to fly up into the airless heights. If somebody didn't come along soon to hold him in their arms, he was going to evaporate. I said to him that we could live together, that I would fill his shoes each morning with all my clinging, heavy, insistent thoughts so that he could go out and dance without succumbing to the call of the skies. Securely tethered to my love, he could float in the breeze without being carried off, swaying among the evening stars as darkness fell, a moon-dancer. And if he wanted, I would loosen the string so that he could take flight, but I would always be the one holding the end tightly in my hand. I would always be the one tying him down.

＊

Illness has made her so thin that making love has become painful. Painful for us both. I wish she could be blooming again, bursting with health, big, full of life. But she's dying and I hurt her. But she's dying and she hurts me.

＊

I left because, for him, only math counted. Yes, counted. That's the word. And me, as for me, I was nothing. I didn't even know my times tables by heart. He thought that math was at the origin of the world, of all its order and beauty. He used to tell me about mathematical formulas that make the impossible possible simply by shifting our point of view. Nothing could escape them. General relativity, quantum mechanics, computer science, chemistry, biology: the formulas ruled them all. I used to put my arms around him and say I'm here, you know. He would say, without math, my darling, you wouldn't exist, neither you nor your words. You wouldn't even be a theoretical possibility. Nothing would exist, you see. Nothing would make the slightest bit of sense, not the double helix structure of DNA, nor the topology of the universe, nor the structure of proteins, a football, or a stray soap bubble. From math, we come to understand our universe, our time, even our emotions. I asked him how he could be so sure and he would smile and say

You don't understand, math wasn't invented by humankind. All we invented was a way of expressing what little we understand of it. Math predates humanity. The least we can do is respect the logic of what we see before us. When he can't work something out, he tries to come up with a theory, to imagine an answer. He must have done that in order to find a mathematical explanation for my departure, some kind of cast-iron equation.

✹

Each time I see him our bodies gently untie their ligaments, unfasten their joints.

✹

She's as clumsy as can be. Still, she prides herself on being in charge of things at home, and she doesn't want me to get involved. She can't mend anything without pricking herself, and her stitching is such a mess it looks like scars. On the hems of my pants, I wear the reminders of her injured fingers, her blood-spotted attempts to be a housewife.

✹

I packed her suitcase just as I always had, as if it was any other trip. I packed two, to be exact, because she was going to be away for a longer period, because she wasn't actually coming back. I put in a few changes of clothes, of course, and also her books. I put in the books she's reading at the moment, the ones she's planning to read soon, and the ones in a pile on her bedside table. Her toiletry bag, as usual. No towels because he's sure to have plenty of those himself. What about medicine? She said Yes, he's already got everything at his house. Sheets, food, dishes. He'll have all that, obviously. Her passport, a bit of money. She said she didn't need money, that she would come back and get all the other things, and I should stop worrying, I was crazy to worry, to be packing her suitcases, I didn't have to do that. But I wanted to. It was what I'd always done.

*

I was walking along, sticking stubbornly to my path despite the distant sound of hunters' guns going off and disturbing my reverie. They were getting closer. From time to time one of their dogs ran past me, its bell ringing, and scampered tunefully ahead for a while before disappearing, sometimes in the direction of a staccato call and sometimes for no obvious reason, perhaps following the scent of nearby game. There were a few sporty types on mountain bikes and some joggers who, like me, were out braving the start of the hunting season. We were a determined, almost militant, few. A bell tinkled behind me and I expected another dog to come trotting past, but what I saw made me stop in my tracks. There behind me, then alongside, then in front, was a man with a bell on his belt just like the ones the dogs wore. Perhaps it was to avoid getting shot by the hunters. He turned around and, still bouncing musically on the spot, asked if he had given me a fright. I didn't answer, beginning to be charmed by the sound of his panting mixed in with the jingling. He bent over with his hands on his knees, trying to catch his breath, and the bell fell almost silent, drawn in toward his body, hunched there, barely two paces away.

✳

We met each other the old-fashioned way through mutual friends. We lived together for fifteen years, had three children, shared friends, joys, holidays, houses, towns, journeys, sadnesses, reconciliations, fears, dreams, and as many memories as you'd care to imagine. He left me because I wasn't up-to-date anymore. He had signed up for a dating site where women choose men and put them in a basket. That's what he said, that he'd been chosen online, and that he loved this modern, dynamic woman.

✳

She can't stand there to be the slightest bump in the bed, even under the sheet. If there's a bit of sand, a crumb, a seed, anything that means she can feel a little lump, she can't sleep. I say she's my princess with the pea, and go and shake the sheets out of the window.

✳

The oil paint never came off, even in the shower. She always had traces of it on her hands, her arms, her face, her neck, and in her hair. Patches of color, bizarre face paint, clashing streaks, clumsy makeup. One evening she came home so clean and so pale, I thought she must be ill. She'd stopped painting a few days before.

✳

He was leaning against the wall, his shadow rippling over the edge of the pavement. I stepped in it.

✳

The real estate agents never notice a thing, nor do the landlords. We make love in their apartments, we sleep in them, we live our shared life in them, and it's as good a life as any. We change location, move to a different town, every day. We leave early in the morning after a quick shower. We get dressed, I put my makeup on, we go out, take the bus or the train, leave our things in a locker at the station, and then look around the new place, the new town and, toward the end of the afternoon, we go and visit apartments arm in arm like a young couple in love, which is what we are. We arrange "open visits," where they give us the keys. We do a little bit of shopping, go back to the lockers, collect our things, and go to the new apartment, which is often empty or sometimes partly furnished. One of us takes the key back to the real estate agent while the other stays in the apartment, settles in, has a bath if there's any hot water, and prepares a cold meal with no cookware. The water is never cut off, the electricity only rarely is, and in any case there's always some light from the street. The one who returned the key comes back. If it's a Saturday we have the luxury of two nights.

✳

She's standing on the beach, reading, and digging down into the sand with small, regular movements of her ankles and toes. I lie down at her feet and, soothed by this gentle shifting which echoes the sound of the waves, fall asleep.

＊

After she left, as though I wasn't sad enough already, I surrounded myself with things that make you cry. Music, first: enough minor keys to drown in, with all their tear-jerking power, and then evening walks by the river. I would go down to the water in search of that special fragmented light, seeking those places where the vegetation is so dense that light can only enter obliquely, prostrating itself to slip among the low branches of the trees that brush the bank, and where the only rays that ever penetrate are those of twilight. I needed things like this, ending, declining, plaintive, and weary, to be able to explore my pain to the full.

＊

He takes photographs of the clippings when I cut my nails, the little hairs left on the strip after I wax my legs, the dead hair in my comb.

＊

I made an inventory of our presents. Mine to him: a boxed set of wood samples, a teapot, a doll, books, books, books, and handmade paper for drawing. His to me: shoes, a blouse, a little blue bird on a spring, books, books, books, and Japanese notebooks for writing in.

＊

When my husband died a few weeks ago I went to his office to sort out his things. He had never let me go there when he was alive but I didn't hesitate for a moment, or even feel guilty. I'd always known there was another woman, right from the start, but I never said anything. As long as he stayed with me I didn't ask any questions, preferring to close my eyes to it. When he died, though, I wanted to know who she was and if I knew her. I wanted to go and see her, introduce myself, tell her he was dead, talk to her about him.

My husband was a poet. Not a real one, or at least, I don't really know. He wrote but didn't publish, or hardly. It was all private, but he did write an awful lot. He would write for several hours each day or each night, whenever he had time, before work, after work, whenever. Any spare time he had before or after, he'd be there, writing, in the room he called his office that was out of bounds to me. It was a rented room on the other side of town. I hardly ever used to see him and he always claimed to be "writing." It didn't take me long to see that writing was an excuse, an alibi. He wanted to go to that room, a few kilometers away from where we lived, to see her.

When I went there, though, I didn't see any traces of a woman, nothing lying around, none of the telltale signs or smells I was expecting. There wasn't a single long hair or a hint of perfume. There was just a table, manuscripts, books, pens, reams of paper, a chair, a few dishes, a fridge, and a big metal chest. So he really had been writing. I opened up the chest, which was sitting in the corner, under the window. There she was, the other woman, in this old traveling trunk. It was stuffed full of thick envelopes addressed to her. He had written thousands of long letters to her over the course of fifty years, since before we were married right up until two days before he died. I read them, every single one, all those tens of thousands of pages with the date at the top on the right. It took me several weeks to read them all. Now I, too, came to the office every day. I know his handwriting and his way of speaking inside out, and I rediscovered them in these love letters that were like poems, and weren't like anything he had ever written for me. She was, he said, his only love, always had been, always would be. She was as blonde as I am brown, or as I was brown before I went gray. He could tell her everything, he wrote, she was the only person to whom he could say whatever he wanted. Reading them, reading those letters one by one, all jumbled up, hurt me, perhaps more even that the fact that he was gone. I'd thought this affair didn't matter to me as long as he stayed, as long as he was near me, but now he was dead, he wasn't near me anymore. The letters were very beautiful. I would read them and cry, feeling that I was losing him all over again. He wrote that he wanted her to destroy the letters and leave no trace behind. But they hadn't been destroyed. They were here, in this trunk, in my hands. When I had finished the last letter, I closed the lid. I didn't need to make a note of her address; I knew it by heart, having seen it so many times written, like the letters, in my husband's writing on all the envelopes. I left the room and when I got home I reserved a ticket online.

Today I'm ready, determined. With a useless map in my hand, I set off in search of her road in a town two hours by train from where we live. The road isn't on the map. I stop some passersby to ask them about the road and about her, because it's a small town and I wonder if they might know her. On the train back, my mind is filled with sudden, urgent questions, questions that hadn't occurred to me before I set off on my search. I wonder why the letters are all in the chest in his office and not at her house, where they should be. Perhaps they had parted and she had returned the letters to him. But he had written to her a couple of days before he died, and even that letter was in the trunk. And why were there no replies, no letters from her? Instead of going back to my house, our house, I go to the office, open up the chest, and look at the envelopes. Not one has a stamp or a postmark. I understand now. I remember whole passages of his writing, parts that he had given me to read. I know his writing, his turns of phrase, so well. Yes, I understand. I understand that actually I had no idea, that what I thought I knew was all in my imagination. This woman doesn't exist. She has never existed except in his head, and in mine. She was his workshop, his way of finding and refining his style, perfecting his voice, developing his thoughts. He could tell her everything; she was the only person to whom he could say anything he wanted. And for a good reason. She replied, or so he believed, so he told himself. She never let him down. He asked her to destroy the letters so that no trace of them was left behind, but in fact he had carefully preserved every draft.

✴

He wears a wide, thick gray belt with straps on it to protect his back when he has to do heavy lifting at work. I like this fragility. It makes him look a bit ridiculous when he's on the building site and also sometimes at home when he has to bend down in the garden, all strapped in to tend the flowers and the herbs.

✴

I dropped her feather in the park. Perhaps someone will pick it up and wonder what it was doing there, a feather from a bird that definitely doesn't come from this part of the world, not from here, not from this park. I didn't drop it on purpose; it fell out of my bag and when I saw it on the ground I bent down and then thought, no. Even just a few days ago, I'd have rushed to pick it up.

I collected up all her feathers when she left me. I keep them bundled together in my backpack, my old faithful backpack that comes with me everywhere. She had asked me to leave our apartment. She said I could go there by myself one day during the week while she was at work so that I could pack my things without bumping into her. I took my stuff and picked up all the feathers I could find. She used to have them everywhere: arranged into bouquets, in her hair, in glasses and cups, left lying around in every room and in everything. She used them as bookmarks, everything-marks, nothing-marks, all sorts of feathers, crow, eagle, robin, sparrow, even rare hummingbird feathers, tiny and shimmering, which she would endlessly ruffle up and smooth out, all brought back from her travels around the world, her little-rich-girl jaunts. The feathers were the one thing that really annoyed me when we lived together. They were her little foible. I thought they were dirty and didn't like having them scattered around the place. There were even feathers in the freezer. She had thick notebooks, a cross between diaries and travel journals, where she would stick the prettiest ones. She was naive and snobbish. Extravagant. After we broke up I swiped the whole collection and preserved it carefully.

Now, I walk around scattering great handfuls of feathers. These feathers that have been in my bag for months, faded, ruined feathers; I let them fall, or fly away and land wherever the air and chance decide.

＊

We've had an argument. More serious than usual. I left the house and I'm walking, fast, to try to calm myself down.

I'm wearing a velvet jacket and as my arms swish against my body the velvet on velvet rasps a little, like a cell phone vibrating. Every step I take, I think he's calling me.

✳

He was incapable of experiencing a real love story, incapable of living it, or of living in it. He couldn't live within a story that he hadn't written himself. He didn't know how to live. He was always detached, observing. He wrote so well about life that I, gullible reader that I was, thought that to write like that about it, he must have lived it. One evening, after he had come to give a reading in the town where I lived, I told him how much I admired him. I said I thought he captured the reality of life wonderfully. I clutched his book to my heart before placing it in front of him but he didn't lift his eyes as he signed it. Then he handed it back, smiled at me, saw me. I didn't say anything. He had taken forever signing the book. He took forever to come anywhere near me when, later on, I wrote him letters and pursued him at readings and talks. I went wherever he went, following him. He took forever to love me, or to pretend. Because he never really knew how to love me at all. He didn't feel anything. He was clumsy and afraid. I think all I did was reassure him a little. He told me he was a virgin even though he was over forty. I thought I was saving him from a life of loneliness. He would talk about the impossibility of communication between men and women, how it was impossible for words, deeds, or shared lives to break down the barrier of our separate bodies. He said that only literature can leap over that barrier. By writing, he thought he heightened his readers' awareness of all sorts of hitherto barely perceived emotions, sensations, and experiences.

It didn't take long for him to leave me. He went back to his books. He left me so he could write this story, our story, and it was then and only then, as he said in interviews, that it all came back to him, or rather it all came to him: the emotion, sensation, and experience of love, but, he was careful to stress, only so that he could write it down, only for as long as it took to write it.

✳

I watch him sleeping and feel very far away during these long nights of insomnia. I gaze at him, so calm, wrapped up in the bedding. I'm completely alone next to this sleeping man. But there's always that moment, a moment that I think can never possibly arrive, will never actually occur, but which is inevitable, inevitable and wonderful, the moment when he wakes up. He emerges from sleep as from a chrysalis and turns to me, shedding the old skin of his night and saying, are you awake already?

✳

He was driving me out to visit a house a few kilometers away from the real estate agency where he worked. I had kept my coat on. We were discussing the price of the house and the possible cost of the work to be done when suddenly he interrupted me and said that he knew me, or rather that he recognized me. He'd seen me in a film, a home video. He asked me if I had a little boy about ten years old who had shared his ice cream on the beach by the lake last summer with a little girl around the same age, and if I had a Calvin and Hobbes towel. The little girl was his daughter, in the middle of the frame, and my little boy was next to her, holding out the ice cream. I was in the background watching, smiling, shy, and chilly-looking in my cartoon towel. He had filmed the whole scene and now here I was, still as shy and chilly-looking, in his car.

✳

We had started arguing in the street and were still at it in the entryway, and then on the stairs. I was trying to explain something that wasn't easy to put into words. He opened the door to his apartment then shoved it closed before I could go in, leaving me on the landing, my words severed by the slammed door.

✳

She lives in the apartment above mine. I disturb her, as she keeps telling me. She leaves me notes, terse little notes, quite rude ones sometimes. She threatens to call the police. I play the saxophone every day. It's my job. I'm a professional saxophonist, but I do use a mute. I'm not, as she likes to describe me, a nuisance. She calls it noise pollution. I call it music. Muted music. Sometimes, yes, I admit, sometimes I do take the mute off, but not for long. I allow myself this luxury when it's a sunny Sunday afternoon, never during the week, and nobody in the building except her ever complains. The other neighbors actually open their windows on those days, the unmuted days, those sunny days when I don't play scales or exercises but just improvise, days when I give mini-concerts on the balcony, which most people enjoy. One afternoon, and, okay, it wasn't a Sunday, a friend wanted to show me a phrase, a little motif, just for two minutes without the mute. She was down here like a shot, really angry. She said Even with the mute I can't stand your music and I can't stand you. The next day she sent her boyfriend down, presumably to scare me. As if I'd fight about music. As if music was something you fight about. He threatened me. I shrugged my shoulders. She wants to file a complaint about neighborhood noise.

It has to be said that her apartment isn't always completely silent. Her bed makes an awful, sad sound in the night when her boyfriend's over. They always screw to the same rhythm, and as far as I'm concerned it's definitely screwing, not making love, because it's always the same dogged, dreary, binary rhythm. The rhythm's the same and the sounds are the same; same tessitura, same component parts. It's always in the same place, in bed, always the same movements, the same cadence, and the same one-sided grunts: his. But I don't go running up there, I don't complain, I don't write her nasty little notes, and sometimes I even say to myself it's no bad thing. I'm in bed, dropping off to sleep, they're up there screwing, and I think, well, at least it's something. They're human beings and they're doing something human. I'm happy for them. I'm not going to call the police. It would just be good if they mixed it up a bit sometimes, if the rhythm and all the rest of it could just be more varied. I'd like to hear her voice sometimes, too, her sounds, because I've only ever heard her when she's annoyed. I worry about her, my upstairs neighbor.

Tomorrow it's going to be a sunny Sunday afternoon. I'll take my mute off. She'll come down right away. I'll open the door and I'll say great, I was hoping she'd drop by so I could talk to her about rhythm, music, modulation, song. I'll tell her to sit down, make her a cup of tea, offer to play her my music, my own music, full of variation. I'll tell her to let herself go, be carried by my breath, my sax, my mouth, my lips, my melody.

✹

When she left me, I cried so much I became truly disgusting, full of phlegm. I began to wonder why tears are the only excretions we don't find repulsive. Perhaps because they're transparent—but then what about saliva or sweat? My tears came with snot, slobber, convulsive hiccups, and a torrent of ridiculous thoughts, of stupid questions.

✳

When she came back from the movie theater she was so tired that she went straight to bed without even putting her clothes in the laundry basket. I kissed her, picked up her things, emptied the pockets, and couldn't help smiling when I found the ever-present handkerchief inside. Usually, I find her habit of using an old-fashioned hanky revolting. It was still warm; I unfolded it and sniffed it. It smelled strongly of apple because she'd kept a core wrapped up in it for the whole film, waiting until she could find a trashcan. I breathed it in deeply and then got into bed, putting my arms around her carefully, trying not to wake her. Her own smell, the smell of the back of the neck where I gently nuzzled against her, gradually replaced that of the apple.

✳

How do you tell someone who loves you so much that they don't love you? How can I say that I don't want it, this stifling love, and that it isn't love?

＊

He has invited a group of friends over for dinner. I can tell he's happy and worried at the same time. He insisted on doing all the cooking himself and now he's busy but still attentive, chatty, and smiling. He thinks the food could do with more salt. I don't like much salt so it suits me fine this evening. We don't live together but know each other well enough to be aware that one of us likes lots of salt and the other very little, almost none. He gets up to fetch the salt, says Here it is, go ahead, it needs more salt. His friends agree and pass the salt round. He waits his turn, talking to his guests, and I wait, like the others, for him to eat before starting my own food. The saltshaker finally comes around to him and he starts to use it. The conversation is flowing. Suddenly he stops, turns to me and, without asking, as though it were a familiar gesture between us, puts salt on my food. I protest, perhaps rather too loudly, and he says Oh yes, of course, sorry, clearly embarrassed.

I can't stop thinking about this little incident. Why, after two years, does he still not know that I don't add salt to my food? Perhaps it's the nerves, the guests, the eagerness for everything to go well, the mixture of enjoyment and worry. Why would somebody who has absolutely ruled out living together make that seemingly familiar gesture, a very kind gesture, helping someone else before himself? Was it a memory from a former life with another woman? Did he used to do that before, add salt to her food, when he was with her and still believed in the idea of a shared life? I wish

I hadn't said no. I keep seeing his hand poised above my plate, turned toward me, attentive, intimate. I'd like him to add salt to all my food. I'd happily be thirsty after every meal for the sake of gestures like that.

✳

She's so short that she barely comes up to my chest. When we make love, she says Make me bigger, unfold me. When I want to kiss her, I take her in my arms and lift her up, she's so light. I say Climb on, and she puts her tiny feet on mine.

✳

One morning as we were lying entwined in bed, I got right up close to her skin and noticed that some of her beauty spots weren't like the others. They were a slightly different color and texture. I was worried, and she tried to reassure me by explaining that they weren't real. They weren't melanomas, they were tattoos. They loved each other so much, she and this other man, before me, that they got tattoos in the same size and shape as the other's beauty spots. They had the exact same ones, in the same places. I got up, and said that beauty spots aren't like tattoos. They change with age and they're affected by the climate. Some of them go away, new ones appear. Theirs probably weren't even the same anymore.

*

We went away for a romantic weekend. We hardly knew each other but already he wanted me to sign my name on the postcards he wrote to his friends, his family, even his beloved old mom.

*

He didn't hear me when I came back into the apartment. He doesn't know I'm here. I thought I'd called out loudly enough but when I saw him I realized he was wearing earphones. I watch him for a long time. He's doing the little things you do when you're alone. Little aimless things: fiddling about in the kitchen, humming, bobbing around.

*

She was talking on the phone in the street, walking slowly and blundering slightly as though she were tipsy. She was distracted by the sad conversation she was having, something difficult and upsetting. She was crying now, and obviously breaking up with somebody. I followed her, listening. She didn't notice, absorbed as she was in ending it with this invisible man whom she said she still loved. When she hung up, I offered her a package of tissues.

✳

He is black-skinned, dressed entirely in black, slim, very elegant, with black sneakers, too, the same black as his clothes, except for flashes of bright yellow that glance up from his soles as he walks. I can't reconcile these intermittent yellow flashes with the rest of him. They seem like a slipup, an error of taste. He walks past me and goes into the corner store next to where I'm standing. He reemerges with a few provisions in a bright yellow plastic bag, the same yellow as the soles of his shoes.

✳

I had a wart on the index finger of my left hand. He found it so repulsive he wouldn't hold hands with me. Every day he told me I should have it removed. The doctor said it wasn't serious and I should ignore it, but I insisted on having it burned away. It turned into a funny little shriveled thing, white at first, then brown, and then it dropped off. It left no trace, no scar at all. A few weeks later he took my hand and told me he had met someone else. That same evening, a little patch appeared in the same place and slowly, day by day, my original wart came back.

＊

It's hard to define this sadness that settles like dust in my mind whenever I stop moving. It isn't exactly sadness, more an oppression that makes my breathing irregular, my body feel awkward, and the afternoons seem interminable. It isn't easy to pin down and it isn't all that bad. On some days it's quite bearable and I almost get used to it. It's just a little too persistent. I have to live with it, since I don't live with him anymore.

＊

Mosquitoes love her skin. Yesterday by the river she smeared herself all over with citronella but they still found a place, a narrow strip above her left foot that she must have missed. The bites make a sort of anklet.

＊

She left last summer without explaining why, leaving her bike leaning against the wall in the courtyard. I got a text saying that I could keep the bike because she wouldn't be coming back. I didn't dare touch it. The courtyard wall is built from large blocks of beige limestone and the gaps between them have gotten deeper over the years. The left handlebar was jammed into one of these cracks. I ended up moving the bike because I got a letter from the tenants' association complaining about it. I pulled the handlebar out and the bike, free of its support, seemed heavy. I put it away in the cellar and came back to have a look at the wall. I couldn't identify the exact crevice which had propped up the bike. There were too many of them, so many chalky fissures in this old wall. I had an urge to push little pieces of paper into them, each with my dearest wish written on it, the same wish every time: make her come back. This wall in the courtyard of my apartment building was like a smaller, more ordinary version of the Western Wall in Jerusalem, the Kotel, where people leave notes with prayers written on them. I prepared dozens of little supplications and filled the wall with my screwed-up sadness.

Last week the owners had some work done on the building and the lovely old courtyard wall was covered in a thick layer of paint that filled in all the cracks.

*

I went to visit him in prison with our youngest daughter. The security scanner was on the blink. It was far too sensitive and detected our humiliation three times. I'd already taken off my shoes and my belt but I then had to undo my bra, because of the underwire. I slipped it off under my shirt and passed it to the security guard, who folded it and put it underneath my coat in the tray. He seemed embarrassed and didn't say anything. Only the scanner spoke. My wedding ring, embedded in the fat of my finger after more than thirty years of marriage, set off my shame once more, but even with the help of a bit of soap the silent guard gave me, I couldn't get it off. They let me through anyway. Behind me, I heard beeping as the braces on my daughter's teeth activated it again. I hated him, then, for stealing those things, for getting caught, and for making us strip right down to our breasts, our joints, our teeth.

✸

She got her revenge for my infidelity by revealing something very private about me to the whole village, a secret about my body that I'm ashamed of and only she knows, because only she knows me properly. Nobody except her has ever noticed my embarrassing little anomaly, not even my mistress, who was always so inattentive, so distant. She made leaflets with an enlarged photo of my defect and a caption announcing my name, and placed one in every mailbox in the village.

✸

He's a saxophonist. I organize his schedule, pack his bags before a tour and, just before each concert, I prepare his instrument. I get out the sax, caress it, bring it to my lips, and dampen the mouthpiece.

✳

Mr. Dickens is right; my husband did not die in those conditions. It is simply impossible. I cannot have done all that I did only for him to be remembered in such a hateful way. I am an influential woman and my husband was already old, not as high-ranking as he would have liked, and frankly very bitter. As for me, I loved him. I loved him so much that I made discreet use of my influence to arrange for him to travel far away and return a hero. I worked secretly so that he might undertake this final expedition, which would assure his lasting reputation: he would find the Northwest Passage. He never knew of my intervention, of course, for I would not have dreamed of tarnishing his glory.

It is claimed that my husband and his team resorted to cannibalism in the attempt to survive. My friend Charles Dickens, the eminent author, whose reliability is beyond question, has stoutly denied these horrible rumors. I am entirely of his opinion, and shall admit no truth in such disgraceful talk. Even if one day I am forced to accept that it is true, I shall never admit it, because it was I and I alone who made possible this expedition, this abomination.

✳

She sits reading on the veranda at night, in the light of the bare bulb hanging from the ceiling. Above her hair, moths form a halo, or perhaps they are thoughts flitting out of the book and through her head. Either way, they pulse and gyrate.

✳

He has brought me to this theme park, as though I were a little girl. He wants to share his memories with me. I don't think you can share things like memories or childhood. He holds my hand and is obviously moved to be here, at this faded place built on the site of an old airfield on a feature-less plateau in the middle of nowhere on the hottest day of the summer. I don't feel anything. I only came along to this godforsaken place to keep him company. The wind is sandblasting our legs and the dry heat gives him an excuse to cry, to shed a few tears over this bleak Wild West of a place, overrun by tacky stalls. The piped music can't hide the throbbing of machinery. The inflatable games are outdated and boiling hot to the touch and the ghost train isn't scary, even for children. The ice rink is made of Teflon and the swimming pool is barely more than a mirage, a tease for our hot skin. On the ground, you can still see the traces of painted lines where the planes used to come in to land. Slumped in a chair underneath a few wispy leaves clinging to the skimpy arbor in the picnic area, I'm so bored that, as time creeps by, I begin to watch the gradual movement of the shadows. He's overjoyed. It's all still the way it used to be. I bet it is. I don't know what to do other than readjust my sweaty breasts in my bikini top. I refuse to go on the slide with him.

✳

He's got to use mouthwash every night before going to bed because of a problem with his teeth. I hear him gargling all the way from the bedroom. The water swishing around in his throat sounds like a laugh coming from somewhere deep inside his body and gurgling its way toward me. I go and join him in the bathroom and imitate him. We burst out laughing, spitting everywhere. Our joy splatters the whole mirror.

✳

She creates characters and sets for her shadow theater using tiny, sharp tools: fine scissors, nail clippers, razors, and tweezers, like the instruments that surgeons, computer engineers, and manicurists use. She even has a little hammer. I watch her shaping her materials, the miniature instruments extending her hands and giving her innumerable, many-jointed fingers and extra fingernails. She makes cardboard animals with jointed bodies held together as if by magic, and puppets made of reeds. Their knee joints are brass fasteners, their elbows bent needles, and their flesh scraps of silk. She sculpts with tracing paper, not hiding the sticky tape but making the most of its transparency. I'm fascinated by her sketches and her scores covered in directions for movements, her plans of all the scenes, carefully timed with a metronome, with numbers scribbled all over them. She works standing up, in front of a sort of bare, wooden crate standing on a light box, where intricate shadows appear and disappear, and rare glimpses in the background of her face in silhouette.

✳

With my advancing age and illness, this indelicate, shameless illness, my wife has seized control of my life, my most intimate privacy. She wants to look after my incontinence pads herself because I don't have a handbag, because I would forget, because she's looking for any excuse to pass me one as indiscreetly as she possibly can, all the while pretending to be discreet and attentive. At a restaurant, for example, she'll pass one under the table, making sure that she says Here you are, loudly enough for everyone to hear, and faking an embarrassed smile for the benefit of the other diners once she's made sure that everyone's looking. My daughter once asked us, when we were staying at her house, what we wanted for breakfast. My wife said that she wouldn't have any orange juice but that I had to have some because she always got me to drink a little in the mornings for my constipation. She watches me constantly, just waiting for one of my moments of shame, my gas, my daily humiliations. On the slightest pretext, especially if we're in company, she asks if I don't by any chance need to have a poo, darling?

*

I was watching him from the ground floor of the huge glass atrium of the shopping mall. He was wearing a splint on his knee and showing off with his cane like a street performer in a funny hat (which he also had). He was pretending to be an injured clown, moving like a floppy puppet abandoned by its puppetmaster. From where I stood, it was like watching a low-angle shot of a marionette dancing. The dislocated movements that he was trying were unintentionally graceful, charming without meaning to be. He threw his cane in the air like an oversized, clumsy majorette. It fell into the glassy void and bounced off the escalator much further down. Next to me.

*

Before I met her I used to talk to myself when I was at home alone. I was a confirmed, finicky bachelor. I had conversations with myself out loud all alone all the time. When she came along, she broke this habit of mine. Since she left there's only silence: the absence of her voice and of mine responding.

✳

I didn't think about what I was doing because I was so absorbed in watching her. I just followed, or rather I overtook her, and opened the heavy car door, holding it open. She stepped out and I did the same. We found ourselves standing like a pair of idiots in a circle painted on the platform with the words "Do not stand here" written inside it. Behind us, the train pulled off again. There was no exit, no tunnel, no escalator or elevator. We didn't dare to get down onto the tracks. We stood there for a few minutes, tight together in the painted circle, smiling, uneasy. Another train stopped and we thought we might be able to get in and use it as a bridge to the other platform, but the doors didn't open on our side. Through the windows we could see all the passengers getting off on the right side.

✳

Whenever I used to make the mistake of complaining, my grandfather would say A good walk will set you right. I was on vacation at their farm. I missed my mother. I had a stomachache from drinking the milk still warm from the body of the cow. I was bored morning, noon, afternoon, and night. He would barely shrug his shoulders: A good walk will set you right. It was brusque but very affectionate and sometimes it was true, a good walk did set me right. It set right tears, stomachaches, even boredom. On the farm, when my grandfather was young, before I came along with my precious city-girl whining, when they hurt themselves a little bit, or even a lot, they carried on. They used to walk, sometimes all night, to take the animals to market. They walked whether they were ill or not, carrying on mowing, milking, tending. They called it tending, not feeding.

Early this morning I remembered that old phrase of my grandfather's when I read the note he left me: I'm going. Don't hate me. Don't call me. It was still dark. My grandfather died a long time ago. I packed my backpack and took a map at random from the shelf. It was a map of the nearby caves. I could get there on foot. I walked without stopping and here I am, already at the mouth of the caves. I take another look at the map to check my path. The paper is all torn and messily folded. I'll patch it up. I'll put Scotch Tape over the worn folds. That map will carry the pain and the memory of pain, the scars of the walk.

✸

His breathing, even during the day, even when he's busy doing something, is like that of a person asleep. Regular and calm. I like this peace.

We were sitting in the noisy, tiered seats. The amateur actors were all either overdoing it or underdoing it. It was painful to watch. I was trying to salvage some enjoyment from the whole thing by imagining attenuating circumstances. She was sitting near me but I'd hardly noticed her. She was obviously bored, to the point of losing her sandal. She jiggled and shifted her whole body in her seat so much that the sandal fell onto the stage. Then I did see her, everybody did, blushing and trying to disappear into her folding chair, trying to hide her embarrassment. Nobody dared to pick up the little shoe, or even move it. It stayed there in the footlights for the whole play. During the awkward applause I ran to fetch it before she could. She straightened herself, got up, then sat down again when I knelt in front of her. I took her bare foot, her summer foot, in my hands that hadn't even had the time to applaud, and I put her sandal on.

✳

Since our son was born, she's had a line of hair stretching from her pubic bone to her navel, sharp and black like an upside-down exclamation mark. I lie alongside her top to tail to read this bravo and answer its call the right way up.

*

She was only with me to have somewhere to write to, an addressee.

*

The only time I dare look at him face-to-face is in the mirror, when we're both getting ready in the morning. We get up at the same time and both enjoy this closeness while we go through our little morning routine. We're far apart all day, out at work, and in the evening we don't manage to talk or look at each other, or even listen to each other. I sometimes watch him surreptitiously while we're eating. In bed, when we're asleep or making love, we close our eyes. I'd like to see him but he prefers darkness and touch. In the morning I can finally look him in the eyes but only via his reflection. I see his face and mine; I can't avoid seeing my own face, watching him, if I want to see his. But I'm used to this indirectness and I no longer notice my own gaze. I only see him, now. And this man in the mirror smiles at me.

*

While the children and I waited for her, we often used to play games. She came back later and later, after we had already played several rounds of Uno or Tri-Ominos. We barely lifted our watchful eyes from the game. She bent down to give us a kiss but we wanted to finish the round first, going counterclockwise, and whose turn was it again?

✳

The man in the market stall picks up an apple and explains to me that the red mark on the yellow skin of the Chanteclair is caused by a moonbeam. It's so early that the sun has barely risen and I'm the first person at the market. The pink-orange color is from the moonlight falling on the side of the apple turned toward it during the night. I don't believe a word of this but I smile, half-mocking, half-charmed, and the same color appears on his glowing cheeks.

✳

When he left me I cried so much that two marks appeared under my eyes, below the rings. Two little purplish bulges where the blood vessels had burst.

＊

I loved him for his hands, right away. He was the first man in my life who shook my hand. The others, whether they were friends or not, gave me a kiss.

＊

I start to undress her and she lifts up her arms to help me. I'm surprised to see a downy layer in her armpits. It's a very light blue, almost gray, almost white. I wonder what planet she's from. I stroke her soft, colored underarms for a long time, before moving on to her ordinary, flesh-colored thighs and stomach. In the morning she dresses lazily and I have time to watch her do it, to notice the fluffy, light blue sweater that she wears next to her skin.

＊

With her I'm finally experiencing a new emotion, or perhaps a renewed one. It's rather like feelings I had as a child, those infatuations unclouded by the sexuality that was to hit me like a weight with the onset of adolescence. They were raw emotions, which seemed then as though they would last for-ever. I had thought they were long gone, were so diluted in my adult self that I didn't think about them anymore. I had my banal, consensual love affairs, muddied by half-expressed feelings, increasingly permeated and burdened by desire. And then I met her. This woman whose life has become a daily cycle reduced to an utter simplicity, freed from expectation but not desire, sometimes gripped by sadness but more often animated by joy, who is the same age as my grandmother. It's her age that allows me this feeling, like my childhood loves. We talk endlessly, dance together, and walk along holding hands.

＊

She lives deep in the forest and hardly ever emerges. She's so pale that to me she always seems to come from another season.

＊

I've just read his note, telling me he's leaving. I found it carefully folded and placed, almost hidden but not quite, in the pile of sheets in the closet in our bedroom. He left this morning. I thought he was working in the field. I wonder why he didn't put it on the kitchen table. Perhaps he wanted to give himself a bit of time, or to give me some. I think he knew I was going to do a white load and that the sheets would be dry by the afternoon. I'm standing here in front of the open closet, the note in my left hand and the sheets draped over my right arm, not knowing which to put down first.

＊

I follow the line with my index finger. It runs up his penis like the tie underneath a tongue. He speaks to me.

＊

He had a strange obsession. He sometimes thought he could smell a special smell coming in through the open car windows. It only ever happened in summer, in all sorts of different places. He would often shout That's it! make me stop the car, and shoot out as fast as he could.

＊

I took him to the station. It was over at last. I didn't love him anymore and I thought I was relieved. On my street when I got back, I saw a girl in tears on her phone. She was telling whoever it was that she still loved them. She stayed there, leaning against the wall near the door of my building. I went up to my apartment on the fourth floor.

It was hot, so I opened the windows wide to let in some air. The girl's tearful words floated up through my kitchen window. She was breaking up at the same time as I was, except that she was crying and she didn't want it to happen. I listened to her until I began to cry myself, until I, like her, still loved him.

❋

Because she's so short, she never stands with her feet flat on the floor in my apartment. When she needs to open a cupboard or take something off a shelf she stands on tiptoe, a ballet dancer delivered to my door. Sometimes that isn't enough, so she perches on stools, chairs, tables, the bathtub, or the bed. She climbs around the place using door handles, window ledges, and open drawers as handrails.

❋

After I had saved a seat for myself with my bag, I left the church to make a phone call before the concert started. When I came back there was a big coat on my chair, still warm from the body that had just abandoned it. I held this shed skin of a man in the air, looking around me, but as no one came to claim it, no one seemed to notice, and it was cold in the church, I wrapped myself up in its abandoned warmth. I was enveloped in this warmth when he came back and found me, and he looked surprised and taken aback. We were both embarrassed. He sat down a little ways off, leaving me his coat and his warmth. That warmth has never left me.

＊

He chose me, so I must be rare, perhaps even precious. He says: No, it was you who chose me.

＊

I never knew if he really loved me or if I was simply the only one. The only one not to be disgusted. He's obese, and was more or less a virgin and completely alone when I met him. His few girlfriends, approached after stubborn and impassioned courtships, had quickly given up searching for masculine attributes in his gigantic body. His penis is tiny, just a very few centimeters long when it's erect. He can't penetrate anything, any orifice, barely a mouth. He can't enter anybody. He has the feeling, though, that everybody else enters him every time they stare curiously at him. He used to say Because of all this blubber I have no privacy, ever. I'm a monster. It was difficult to masturbate him; I had to rummage around in his stomach, plunging my hands into the fat. But there was no rush and I was patient and determined. I loved him. Loving him allowed me to touch him and to gaze at him for a long time. An enduring gaze effaces imperfections and a tender touch exorcises anything frightening from a body. His was no longer made of rolls of fat, but became a landscape. My eyes and fingers could roam over endless folds, which hid treasures that nobody before me had ever wanted to discover. I felt as though I was penetrating him, entering him, though not violently. With his permission. His intakes of breath, his desire, his hands on the back of my neck gave this permission without fear. He trusted me. I managed to take his penis between my thumb and index finger and it was like picking a delicate flower. I tried to seize the stalk at its base, as near as possible to the earth, its root. I plucked his pleasure at its source. Sometimes he was so relaxed and calm that he stretched out, opened up, and then I could entwine his penis with my tongue, that penis that was also a sort of tongue. We could speak to each other wordlessly with our lips, his made of the fat that was all around his penis, mine slightly dry and covering my teeth because I was afraid of hurting him. I was in love with a man who had lips around a penis that was like a tongue, a man whom nobody had ever before had the patience to bring to orgasm. It was this patience that responded to, and was as immense as, his endless waiting, the waiting that I mistook for love.

✳

The skin of his face creases up; his smile finally appears, fleeting as a timid fish piercing the surface of the water.

✳

His kisses weren't kisses, but smooches instead, like the play kisses a child might give you on the cheek or the neck. They made a silly, smooching sound and were very unpleasant. He wasn't a child, much less mine. He kissed me like that all over, making a loud noise, without tenderness, without desire, playing.

✳

He left with just one suitcase. For weeks afterward I couldn't even think about looking after the children or the house. I couldn't think about anything. Barely managed to eat and drink, or notice if it was raining outside. Then the children got sick of the dirty dishes and canned food. They said I had to snap out of it and tried to help me make a start. Start on what? Do what? That's what I said to them. There are so many things to do.

I know it rained today. I know that for sure because I went outside to hang up the laundry and then went back out almost immediately to bring it in again. Tomorrow, when the sun has dried the ground under the trees, I'll collect some kindling before the rain turns into snow so that I can light the boiler this winter without having to chop the logs that he prepared. I prefer bundling up the wood to chopping it. I'd rather walk around and gather twigs than hack away with tools that could really hurt me, tools he's held in his hand. My hand has lots of scars. I'm so clumsy.

There's everything still to do in this house, or nearly. I could make a list and get organized but it would be so long and where would I start? There are all these things to do before the cold weather comes: finish insulating the attic, bring in and put away the twenty or so cubic meters of beech logs that were delivered yesterday, put the French window in, tidy up the mess he left in the two workshops, and all these things to do before I lose the will to do them—lay a new wooden floor over the old one, nail down the paneling in my youngest son's room, sort out the last few electric cables still dangling in the kitchen, go to the dump and empty the trailer, lay the rest of the tiles on the ground floor, not to mention the everyday things, laundry for three children, meals, housework, and just when I've got all that to do this summer as well as trying to forget him, all of a sudden I get the urge to sort out the big heap of rocks. Sitting on this little avalanche of stones, behind the house, I can see all the trash that has been chucked in there over the years, just like it has in all the rock piles around here. Getting rid of this trash suddenly seems absurdly more important than all the other jobs. There are old packages from animal medicines in there, cow syringes, lone shoes, glass bottles, car batteries, gas cans, all the neighbors' trash from the time when it wasn't just a few neighbors but a village, a village of several hundred inhabitants. I live here alone now, alone with my three children.

Clearing out the rock pile has become my priority. The task is infinite, like the time it will take me to forget him.

✳

She inspects herself in the mirror from every angle, seeking imperfections. She doesn't find any, and leaves the bathroom feeling pleased and beautiful, but the mirror can't reflect something that lies just beneath the skin, something that is there, inside her, that prevents us from loving each other, that she will never see.

✳

He caught me while he was out fishing. He says fishing means taking what comes your way, casting the bait, casting your eyes over the water. Fishing means contemplation and solitude. He's crazy about fishing, he really caught the bug. I took his bait one morning when he saw me hesitate and then wander into his solitude. I was walking on the other bank. I'd strayed off the path, gotten lost, and moved toward the distant sounds of a breeze and moving water: a river that would help me find my bearings. I continued along the bank and our eyes met over his line.

＊

I designed my own kitchen using special software. The furniture and decor in my apartment are very important to me, particularly my kitchen, where I eat breakfast. I need to wake up in a sober, functional, attractive space, a reflection of my own inner space, my mind. I think IKEA is my favorite store.

I was with a girl who disrupted my rituals, my morning rituals. I felt as though Big Brother were watching me in my own kitchen. Because I loved her I tried to break away from the rituals, but that wasn't enough. She continued watching me, analyzing me, dissecting and criticizing my every little habit point by point. When my mornings reverted to their usual solitude, it took me an extremely long time to recreate my rituals, and it was very disconcerting not knowing how to begin the day.

＊

I used to sniff her all the time. Odors are always stronger when they're damp. Perfumers dampen thin strips of paper to sample their scents. Dampening an area, an object, or a body helps us to smell it and get to know it fully. I moistened her all over with saliva to get to know her by heart.

✳

The things I miss most are the sounds, the sounds of our love, the noises of lovemaking and sleeping together, the noises of waking up.

✳

He seduced me by helping to heal a wound that I thought was already mended. I realized later that he always approaches women that way. He seeks the chink, finds it, opens it a little, and pretends to seal it up again. In reality, he dives into the breach and makes it bigger.

✳

She had the dirty habit of putting her hands on the windowpanes when she was looking outside, even when I'd just cleaned them, as though seeing through windows was something done with your fingers. She had little hands. She probably still has them, those little hands, glove size seven, but I can't see them to check. I know she must, as I don't imagine she's changed size, but I can't be sure because she left me. I'm not sure when it was. I don't know how long ago it must be. The marks of her palms and fingertips are still on the windows, clearly visible when I put my mouth up close and exhale, when I bring them out with my breath. I'm worried that they'll disappear. They're still there, so it can't be long since she left. But the windows are getting grubby and they need cleaning. My friends say I should pull myself together and stop letting things go. It's about time to do a bit of housework, they say, give the windows a wipe, what with all the rain we had last year and the pollen in spring, and the pollution of the city. No, it can't be a year already. Her handprints are still there. None of my friends can explain that, none of them can tell me why her little hands are still on the windows despite all the dust, despite the months and months that have allegedly passed. I know it isn't long since she left. They're tricking me with all that stuff about rain and pollen and pollution. I breathe on the glass and see her there, hands pressed against it, looking out, and just to be sure, when I'm alone, I fix her prints to the window with hairspray.

✳

Her collarbones are keys that I turn with my eyes to open up her body. It works every time.

✳

Mental illness makes her beautiful. Beautiful and mad. I live with him and I'm not ill or beautiful, just ordinary. He says that she fascinates him and that he has to look after her. He's going to leave me for her. She needs him. But I need him too, only I'm not lucky enough to be mad, mad and beautiful.

*

He never looked at me. Not at me or at anyone. He's a photographer. He didn't see me. He didn't see anyone. He didn't take photographs of me, not of me or of anybody, only of the city, a closed city. Rooms without windows, unseeing. He photographed lowered blinds, closed shutters, railings, and enclosed spaces. Those photographs are all I have left of him. I look at them and all I see are closed things, closed openings. Inprisonments. Doors, windows, and storefronts all shut up or barred. Blind photographs. The whole city a recluse. It draws back behind vertical and horizontal bars, as though the images were crossed out in all directions. The gaze is struck through. Barriers of metal and wood stand in prohibition. My eyes come up against shutters and linger on them, straying over their surfaces and edges. These photographs through half-closed lids are the work of a man I loved. He closed his eyes. He looked within and saw so much darkness that it mattered little if the city was actually bathed in sunshine, or if I was smiling. To him, it was all closed.

✳

She can't see it even if she tucks in her chin as far as she can, this single hair growing in the blind spot where her breasts begin, just below her throat. It's dark and wiry, like a chest hair, but longer. She can only see by looking in the mirror and sticking her chest out. She often forgets about it and doesn't pluck it out but I don't say anything. I like the fact that she forgets.

✳

Suddenly I wasn't reading the words in his letter anymore; I was hearing a voice. It wasn't his voice but I did recognize it. It was a voice that could have been an echo of my own. I thought I was in love with him but really all I was looking for was a reverberation, a voice that would amplify my own, which was thin and reedy.

✳

We separated last night. I walked out before dawn with my wheelie suitcase into the streets of this vast southern city with its filthy town center, so dirty and empty, and completely taken over by the mistral, the wind that doesn't freshen anything and is good for nothing but chilling us through, spreading trash around us and hanging garlands of ragged plastic bags in the spindly branches of the trees. The New Year's Eve parties are over; soon it'll be the sales. The actual garlands, mean and sorry-looking, each missing a bulb or two, flicker in this lingering cigarette butt of a night. There is no one on the winter streets; I saw just one other person on foot, a man dragging a tall Christmas tree, off to throw it out, most likely. It's very cold. I pulled my double hood right over, but I still felt the scrape of branches against my head when that man went by. The silence, born of the wind's roar and the streets' emptiness, is invasive, tyrannical; it feels as though the town has gone into hiding, in the wake of a disaster. The mannequins are naked and visionless behind the half-parted steel shutters of a children's clothing store. I stop in front of these baby mannequins waiting for their next outfits. I feel numb, dazed. I have to shake myself and get walking all the way to the station. Tomorrow the storm will break and everyone will flood into the shopping malls. Of the everyday, teeming city, I shall see nothing.

✳

There was a girl my age in the next tent at the campsite. We went to the beach while our parents were having aperitifs. She lay down, tucked away in the hollow of a dune and I sat down close by. She didn't move, she was waiting. I didn't dare move a muscle. It was my first time, my blood numbed me all over, and just when I was about to go for it, yes, I was going to kiss her, I saw hers, between her legs, a steadily growing patch on her pale swimsuit.

＊

I went to the clinic to catch his soul and bring it back home. I had string with me to lead it. A great big ball of thick string. I went up to him, embraced him one last time, rested my lips on already cold eyelids, then took his wrist and tied the string to it, as I had seen my grandmother do with my grandfather's wrist in the local hospital. Then, from this bracelet, I unrolled the ball across the room, down the corridors of the clinic, and out to the parking lot where a taxi was waiting for me. I ignored the looks and questions. I held on to the string through the open car window; he followed me the whole way. I talked to him, telling him to come with me, to come back home. I asked the driver to drive very smoothly so that the string wouldn't get broken. I got out without letting go of the ball, which was almost all gone now, and went into the house. I continued unwinding it all the way into our room, right into the bed. I put the end of the string to bed between our sheets.

＊

She gets a kind of rash from contact with semen, which gives her skin a cute, slightly blotchy look. I wipe it off quickly before the reaction shows, but she often says Leave it, it's not bad, it'll go, it doesn't bother me, it hardly itches. Sometimes the red patches appear even before I come, on her neck and her belly, as though her body is anticipating mine.

✻

He doesn't go to the sea to swim but to collect agates. That is, he sorts through the pebbles, examines them, lays them out in heaps, sorts them again, and examines them again, until he finds that special stone. He contemplates what the waves leave behind. I met him on the beach, looking for his precious stones. I had gone for a run in the earliest daylight, before sunrise. In that glimmering haze, I could just make him out as he approached, and paused, holding something in his hand. I stopped nearby and bent over, to calm my panting. I straightened up. The sun was rising in his palm. As if he meant it for me. The agates were reflecting those first rays. I took this burst of morning light from his hand into mine. He was proud of his find. Every time he comes back home with his treasures, I see that first glimmer once more.

✻

My husband's body is in pieces. He is a parts model, mainly doing ankles, knees, elbows, and wrists. A man of many parts, he also occasionally does skin and the nape of the neck, more rarely he does hands. He has some odd moves. He holds his hands up in the air and keeps them there before shoots, so that the blood drains out and his veins don't show too much. Hands up and shooting, like in a cop film. You have to be in top condition to do skin; he looks after his by watching what he eats. Above all, of course, he looks after his ankles, knees, elbows, and wrists, keeping them toned with a strange, gentle dance, supple gesturings that he has developed for himself by adapting movements from bharata natyam that massage the joints and strengthen the ligaments. He watches his weight: he mustn't grow too thin or his bones will show, he mustn't look bony. He is careful with his posture. Very often, he is assigned to work with other body parts. Sometimes a number of them will make up a single body, one glossy-magazine body, grafted together in Photoshop. When it's just him, then it's for close-ups with swatches of fabric or objects. With sections of makeup applied by body artists, my husband is meticulously cropped by photographers who never see the whole of him, as if, in fashion, the gaze works along dotted lines. At night, in my arms, he comes together again.

✳

He has a way of handling things that instantly tells me the kind of mood he's in, particularly the way he closes the door when he's going out or coming in. This morning's door wasn't a bad one.

✳

One summer when I was young, at a bit of a loss and looking for something to do, I got hired to work on a film shoot not far from our village, in the middle of nowhere. It was the event of the year and all the villagers had managed to get involved in some small way or other; most of them as extras. Extra-excited, that is. I had almost nothing to do. I made a few cups of coffee and stuck orange gaffer tape on the ground when the assistant director told me to, sticky markers that helped the actors to move around, get in position, and be exactly where they were meant to be. Sometimes, depending on what the shooting script demanded, the end of some tape had to be pulled up fast before it could be seen on-camera, in a reverse tracking shot, for example, not that I knew anything about it, but I did know that I had to rush over to the actor's feet to pull up the marker and erase the evidence that the whole thing was staged. So I raced head-down toward him, thirty years ago, and, in my first-timer's fluster, I fell over. I was saved by his ankles, and by his laugh.

✳

When she undressed, the very dark coloring of her areolas surprised me. She has such white skin. She said with a little smile It's been a good while since I've had pink nipples. I didn't know that they'd grown darker with her pregnancies and I didn't know how many children she had. I didn't know much about her or about life.

✳

Just as though we shared the same nerves.

✳

It didn't work out between her and me. I always had another woman in mind, the next one. I thought I would meet another woman, down the line, or maybe even her but better—better because it would be down the line. What do you call that feeling, just like nostalgia except about the future? The regret, the longing to rediscover something you haven't yet lived through? I was pining for that future time and also, in anticipation, dreading its loss. I was living entirely in anticipation. I was awaiting and mourning the non-arrival, the not-yet-happening, of everything. And everything that was already there, at hand, seemed entirely unimportant, seemed not to exist. Even I existed only in the future. She, though, she was in the

present; she was entirely present. Now she's in the past.
I'm waiting for her to come back.

✻

Every evening I carefully pluck hairs from my husband's
back and shoulders. He doesn't like the fact that he's hairy,
especially on his back, because that's the only part of the
body that you can't see, that you can't control. He is very well
groomed and would hate to let himself go. He says to me
Only you are allowed to see my back, my imperfections. So
for ten years now, every evening, this has become our bed-
time ritual. I remove a few of these hairs to which I alone
have access, then I run my hands over his shoulder blades
and down to his waist. I pluck all the hair out, and when, after a week or two, I get to the bottom of his back, it's already
time to begin again at the top.

✻

I was at my desk in the study room at the library, absorbed
in my reading, nicely cradled in the cone of light from my
lamp and in the studious silence, in my bubble as they say.
His shadow moved over me. He was doing the thing I hate,
which I've never let anyone do before: he was reading over
my shoulder. I don't know why, but that time it didn't bother

me. I didn't look at him. After a very brief interval of hesitation and surprise, I started to read again, and so did he, standing there behind me, having shown the delicacy to step back just enough to give me the light I needed and without ever muddying the silence, that silence libraries have, composed of little papery noises, of chairs creaking slightly and muffled steps. His hands settled on either side of mine, which were holding my book; his down-stretched arms were like protective barriers around my space, my jealously guarded reading space, our space from now on. And without needing to see each other, our eyes moved at the same pace, paused in the same places, made the same breaks for commas, and finished sentences in perfect time. I could feel, as I turned a page, that he had read to the end of it. We were reading at the same rhythm, and since then we have taken care to maintain that rhythm, even when things aren't great between us. We still read together, and if we lose each other over a few lines, we wait.

✳

She lives in a house by the sea, at the end of a road that floods at high tide. Twice a day, nature seals off her doors and swallows up her road. I can only go to see her at low tide.

✳

He wraps presents like no one else. Perfect packages, for Christmas or birthdays, neatly taped up, the paper smoothed by the assiduous flat of his hand, with a fold positioned two-thirds of the way along the top side, as if he were ironing a crease into a shirt. That fold is his signature.

✳

I lived with her for so long that we ended up sharing the same ideas about life. Our house, our things, our obsessions, our work, all these shared arrangements, we had them all in place, just so. Some would call this routine; I call it intimacy. The objects in our house, the furniture, ornaments, and books, remained in the same positions and the same rooms for years. I used to know those positions and those places by heart, I no longer noticed them. Last year, something changed, some books perhaps, or the vase in the living room, a chair. Something was out of place, only slightly. I didn't exactly see it, I felt it. I could feel something was out of step, there was a kind of dissonance. I was disoriented. I thought she was going to leave me, that there was someone else, and I started to hunt for signs. In my jealousy I found myself muddling everything, scattering, disordering, destroying our ways, unbalancing our life together for good.

✳

She often went walking. She always had a backpack ready to go. I bought hiking boots so I could follow her. She didn't want me to go along. I stare at these boots that don't take me anywhere, brand new in my cupboard. My stupid boots.

✳

All I did was observe him on the sly, the man next door to my life.

✳

I saw her again much later. On her finger she still wore the emerald I had given her, the color of her eyes. With the passing years her eyes have faded; the emerald hasn't.

✳

He has brought me to a budget hotel and I didn't object. I feel worn out. The winter is too long for living alone. You reach the rooms by an outside walkway that is covered in a thin layer of ice. I have good shoes on, I don't slip. He has city shoes and he slips, he slips and falls in all his cut-price confidence and even that doesn't make me laugh. Everything about him is grim and cheap. We met earlier in the shopping center. He picked me up in his radio-less car and we drove around in search of the cheapest hotel. He was after a "First Class" hotel for us at any cost (not at any cost, actually), but he had left the GPS at home so it wouldn't get stolen. He was telling me these stupid details as he drove, perhaps to fill the awkward silence. He had only bought the GPS so as to have one and because there had been a flash sale the week before. I don't know what a flash sale is but I didn't want him to tell me. He'd just stopped to look at the map. I teased him for being too vain to wear his glasses. He told me to shut up. Our awkwardness was starting to steam up the windows.

While he's getting back up, there, on the walkway, rumpled and lumbering, I remember a favorite little story my mother used to tell and that I was always asking her for. I especially liked it because it didn't have an ending, it was beautiful but sad, the head fireman was crying into his helmet, a teardrop rolled, dropped, and froze, the little prince who was passing by slipped on it and died, there was a splendid funeral, it was beautiful but sad, the head fireman… I hear him cursing the winter. It's sad, but nothing to write home about. It's sad but not in the same way. It's just pathetic. I am angry with myself for bringing this precious childhood memory into it.

We go into the tiny hotel room. The double bed has a loft over it so low that there's no chance of my riding him. He hasn't got an erection. He masturbates a bit but as nothing happens he says he's going to "prepare" himself, indicating a cupboard that he calls the bathroom. I go to the window and look out at the gray ice shining under the lights that have just come on. It's only just six o'clock. It's beautiful, all glittering, you'd think there was quartz left behind in the concrete. I feel as though I've been set free by that metallic chill, so that's what I do, I get dressed and I free myself, into the freshness of the winter evening, and once more without slipping.

✳

When I'm waiting for him, I see him everywhere, and every far-off figure is a new arrival. When he doesn't come, I still think it must be him, and every figure as it closes in is a disappointment.

✳

I pass her every evening on the great flight of stairs that connects the lower half of town to the upper half—those never-ending steps that I used to curse for their endlessness. But since she started coming down them every evening just when I'm going up, it's the moment I live for, all day long, our encounter on the steps. I never dally at work anymore as I had begun to, out of loneliness. She's always on time, too. Sometimes she's out of breath, her hair coming loose and even lovelier, and I can't tell if she's hurried so as not to miss me or if she's had a tough day.

✳

He looked happy to be with me in the museum. I liked seeing him like that, enthusiastic and cheerful; it didn't happen
so often. That day, it seemed he was forgetting her at last, the
girl who still made him so sad, the one before me, the one I
couldn't make up for. He liked the photographs on display
and kept pointing them out to me, saying Look. When we
left he bought a postcard of one of the photos, the caress of
a white hand on a slightly darker chest. At the hotel, while I
was sleeping beside him, he wrote on the card and, the very
next morning, he sent it to the woman he's still in love with.

✳

He was shifting around on his chair in the restaurant,
scratching at his thighs, on top, underneath, in between. It
was embarrassing.

✳

More and more often he would be out of breath when he
walked or laughed, or after making love. For the last few
months he'd felt as though he was suffocating. He had pains
running through his chest and he told me he could feel his

heart pounding through his whole body. The diagnosis was a severe heart condition that would require a transplant. He was added to a list. While he waits for his new heart, he wants to live, to live as fully as possible just in case. And living, he says to me, means walking, laughing, making love. Making love more than anything, sweetheart, don't deny me my life. But I'm afraid. I'm afraid he'll have a heart attack. I refuse him.

✳

Throughout the exam, concentration in the room is so complete that the slightest noise is an imposition. When the watch he has placed on the table falls off, every face is startled and every expression is annoyed, except for mine, right behind him, fixed on the back of his neck and on his body hunched over the paper.

✳

She is a schoolteacher. For years now, in an effort to make herself heard in her classroom full of noisy students, she has been pitching her voice differently. She has done it gradually, working her way into it without even realizing what she was doing. By relaxing and dropping her larynx to talk to her rowdy little bunch, she makes her nasal cavities, her sinuses, and the whole of that part of the face that opera singers call the "maschera" resonate. She's my lady of the mask. I love her voice so much. I am sensitive to all kinds of sounds; I'm a studio technician. I've heard her voice change little by little. When she's teaching, her voice grows louder without her having to shout: she supports her middle register and head voice, her spectrum grows richer, and the sound is brought forward. She modifies her voice depending on whether she's at home or at school. Sometimes when she comes home at night, she's still using her powerful work voice, and then she adjusts it. She goes back to the voice she keeps for us.

✳

Desire for her made me stronger, a good deal stronger than her.

✳

She inspects the contents of her cup without drinking, without speaking. After leaving the courthouse, we have come to this bar for one last coffee together. We are divorced, as of a few minutes ago. Staring into her cup, she contemplates our past and I contemplate her.

*

I love it when he goes around naked in my house. It's as if he lived here.

*

She works in my architectural practice. To be specific, she builds my models. Her fingers are made for it, they're so delicate and tiny. When she bends over our miniature houses, her already tiny and slender body seems to shrink even more, as if to inhabit these compressed spaces. I watch her diminution. One of these days, I'll pick her up in one hand and put her down in a minuscule garden. When I tell her this, she smiles, and her smile is bigger than she is.

*

He controls my whole life, right down to the slightest of my movements. He decides what time I should get up, shower, and eat, if I'm allowed to speak, how I should dress and have my hair cut, where I should walk, and how long I should walk for, which book I should read, if I'm ever allowed to read that is, for as he says, apologetically, Sometimes, my darling, they're too sophisticated for you. He claims to be protecting me. He puts me under domestic arrest. He says there's only one way to love and that's to be faithful, in the medieval sense. He talks pointedly about feudal love. He restricts and compartmentalizes my time and space. He organizes everything as if it were all in a day's work but if, for example, I open my eyes when it isn't time, he wakes up in turn and panics, saying What on earth do you think you're doing? To calm him down I have to conform scrupulously to the timetable he has planned for me and which he has been careful to provide in hard copy: he has presented me with a schedule in which my whole life is set out because, he says Otherwise you'll never be able to manage your life.

✳

When he died, I looked after his family. I loved him so much, more than the women I had loved, more than my parents. He was my friend, my only genuine friend. He had a son who was still young and I couldn't leave his wife to fend for herself. I asked her to marry me. I suspected she had always been a little in love with me and besides, she was sad and felt very alone. I broke up with my partner, even though I was very attached to her, not as much as to him but a good deal more than to his wife. I left a woman I loved for the wife of my best friend, a woman I didn't love, but who had been his wife: his widow, now. It was hard at first: our mourning both brought us together and kept us apart. The little boy seemed inconsolable and she was so easily consoled in my arms that I was outraged. For me, my friend was irreplaceable. After a few years, I began to see her without thinking of him and, little by little, I understood what he saw in her. Now it may be that I love her too.

❋

She puts her arms around me, talks to me, and supports me with her words and her eyes. I cannot respond. So I lie to her. I need her in order to become the man I must become, but I'm not sure I love her.

This is much harder than I had expected. I often dream of stopping, but I see her smiling at me and I can't think straight. I would like her to teach me not to lie anymore, but if I stop lying, I'll no longer be able to tell her that I love her.

❋

It was the day of her humiliation, the worst humiliation of her whole life. The best day of mine. She still blushes now, if we talk about it. Anyway, she prefers not to talk about it, when people ask where, when, and how we met. She was incredibly absentminded then—she still is a bit absentminded, but much less. We were partying, "out clubbing" we used to say, even though it's the polar opposite of going out: being shut away in a dark, smelly room, full of sweat and smoke. I never liked it, but I'd promised a friend Yes, okay, I'll be there, for your birthday, but you won't get me back in a hurry. The first days of good weather were pushing in after a winter that had lingered beyond all reason, and all the hot girls had gotten their miniskirts out. She was there, dancing, in a floaty little dress. Airborne, the dress, the girl. She seemed to be into this: dancing, going wild, breaking out, splitting conventions and expectations at the seams by shaking her hips and all the rest of her. She was twisting her hips around, she had the body for it, supple and slender with beautiful legs. I was going to stop there, just looking, disappointed to be always falling back into the same clichés, the same as everyone else, as dumb as the next guy: the pretty girls dance and the boys look on, while the shy ones, the plain janes, sitting beside them, a glass of something in hand just for show, give up even trying to attract their attention. I was going to stop there, steer clear of that never-ending dance of one-track eyes, as if we were all wearing blinders, when something else caught my attention. This girl, this beautiful girl who was drawing all eyes in the room, far from being ogled for her beauty, was being mocked: one of her legs was hairy, really hairy, just the one. Suddenly I tuned in to my friends' digs, their giggles and crude comments. She must have spent the whole winter in pants, not undressing for anyone, it didn't make sense otherwise, so much hair. She must have gone through some long ordeal of arctic heartache and then, with the return of spring, she had said Enough misery, I need fresh air, to go out, to flirt. But, lord knows why (a phone call from a friend, she told me later), she had forgotten to wax one entire leg and hadn't yet noticed. That is how I fell in love with her, instantly, upset by her huge oversight and then by all that followed, her terrible embarrassment when someone finally told her, her disarray, her flight, and my race to catch up with her.

✳

We have never wept at the same time.

✳

I unfolded the map of the town and saw all the places we used to go, she and I. I used colored pencils to mark out our routes and our habits, to color in our cinemas, our theaters, her swimming pool, my library, our friends' streets, our bookstores, our restaurants, our parks. Onto the map I traced our complete intimate topography.

✳

I went back to the troubleshooting page. This channel doesn't exist. It isn't in any listings, not Télé-Z, nor Télé-7, nor even on Télérama or the Internet. He shrugs. If I press the LIST/ FAV button, which pulls up a list of favorites, it doesn't come up. It doesn't come up anywhere. The troubleshooter gives the following diagnosis: a faulty connection. I look at him. He loves this channel's only program. As soon as he turns on the TV, it shows this stupid program that has him grinning, but if I'm the one who fiddles with the remote, the channel never comes on. I can't find it.

There are people—it's well known—whose mere presence can disable electronic things. I examine his delicate wrist, his hand, that long deft hand that sometimes withdraws in order to run down over my belly, his fingers, those fingers that he knows precisely how to trail over my shoulders, back, or hips, his fingers holding the remote control. I wonder if he's one of those people who interferes with television waves. Or perhaps it's me.

He turns around, puts the TV on standby, and says Come here you, why are you trying to compete with the TV? Stop being jealous of a screen. It's ridiculous. Yet there are some days when he looks to the screen so often that I cease to exist, ever since he discovered that channel, the channel that doesn't appear in any listings guide.

The images speak a language I don't even understand but in which he seems quite fluent, an obsessed spectator, speaking this thin, bare language made up of head shakes and idiotic grins. The screen draws him away from me. That screen, blocking the rays so as to protect our eyes, it's also what picks them up and sends them back out, projects them. It both blocks and projects luminous intensity. I slip into darkness, I sulk, I disappear.

＊

On the train, the man next to me takes a little towel out of his bag. I wonder if it's so he can wash his face in the restroom. No, it's a tiny little towel for going to sleep while on the move. He puts it under his chin, near his mouth, to make it softer, more comfortable, presumably. I see his eyes close and his lips fall slightly open, a drop of saliva runs onto his chin: the towel is there to absorb the overflow of sleep. It falls off when he wakes, and is left behind as he hurries from the train. I catch up with him and give it back.

＊

I'm in love with a rubber-band girl. She has them everywhere on and around herself. They're all over the house, too. On her wrists, like bracelets (ready to be used elsewhere), on her ankles (should one of her socks give up the ghost or in case she has a sudden desire for a bike ride), around her many notebooks (to keep them closed, or to hold in loose sheets), in the book she's reading, as a bookmark (the elastic band runs through the book, cutting into the spine, holding the pages like sections of hair, like two pigtails that only become even when she has read halfway), on chair legs, on door and window handles, around Tupperware containers (even those that close tightly—you never know), around endless packages of anything and everything (you'd be forgiven for thinking that the packages' only purpose is to justify the bands), often in her mouth when she's about to tie something (almost all the time, really), and, of course, in her hair.

※

He's so far away from me that he's no more than an idea in my dreams. He is the very furthest thing there is.

※

We are messing around in the bathtub. Laughing, she tells me off for getting water everywhere, but it's the wrong moment to talk: she swallows the little lump of soap that shoots out of my hand just as I meant to slip it down around her neck. After a nervous silence, she starts laughing again, and blowing bubbles out of her mouth and nose. I kiss her to burst them and join in with her giggling.

※

In the beginning, as a timid newcomer, I allowed myself to fall into the arms he held out to me. I had only moved into the retirement home under pressure from my children. I felt lost and betrayed. He was there, he comforted me, he offered me the solace of a love story at an age when I thought I had forgotten everything about love. When I found my bearings, he left. I'd forgotten nothing about love; it hurts as much as ever. He moved on to a resident who is starting to show signs of dementia and has trouble remembering things. One of the nurses told me to stop crying. She said it wasn't worth it. She has known him for years, and he only latches on to women who are disoriented. He wants them to need him. When they recover a bit, like you, he leaves them. It shows you're doing better.

✳

He dislikes cardboard and plastic packages. As soon as we get back with the groceries, it's Operation Unwrap. All the groceries are sorted into carefully categorized piles on the big kitchen table and then re-homed in glass jars prepared in advance. I sit down and watch him do it, his agile hands systematically sorting, pouring, sealing.

✳

Since I met her, elements have been shifting inside me. From time to time I hear the clicking of moving parts; inside my body, I feel the smooth turning of cogs, all the slow and delicate working of wheels I hadn't even suspected were there. I don't know which sections of me are involved, nor how they are acting upon each other. I listen to these renovations inside my suddenly obedient frame. Something is changing, but what is it? She's amending my body, renewing it from top to bottom, painlessly. She's reshaping me from the inside. All she's keeping is the bone structure and the skin, everything within is being reorganized. I don't understand what's happening.

✻

I didn't try to make her stay. I said nothing, and she seemed surprised by my indifference as she packed her suitcases. I stayed reading in my easy chair, as if her leaving meant nothing, as if everything, all around me, were not disappearing along with her. She said All right, I'm off, and I heard the door open and close. I stayed sitting in the chair, book in hand. I think I even turned a page just then, to continue the sentence I'd begun. Then I felt something warm move against my legs. She hadn't taken her cat. I picked him up by the scruff of the neck and went and drowned him by holding his head in the toilet. He didn't struggle.

✻

He came to my place three times and I loved him as I have never loved before. He didn't come back. It's been several weeks already but I haven't lost my hard-on, I am living in a state of permanent desire. All the rest is sterile: my pointless youth, my ridiculous work. I'm stuck on a vacation with nowhere to go. He only came here three times but that was enough to fill all the space I had. Now my apartment is unoccupied and I sit here in a vacuum, my cock sticking up in the empty space.

＊

He was inaccessible, taken up with his work, his friends, his social life. He never looked at me. Yet we often met. He didn't fancy me, there was no connection. Once in a while he even said Hi, absentmindedly, like I was a nobody, just a stranger you bump into on the street, someone you can't avoid but forget right after. One day a mutual friend spoke to him about me, at my request: no, really, he had no idea who I was. I didn't give up, though. I took advantage of his blindness to me to research and to learn everything about him: his past, his present, his family, his apartment, his work, his circle of acquaintances, his tastes, everything, from his little obsessions to the so-called secrets of his childhood, so that eventually nobody could ever have known as much about him. It was as if I were all his old friends and his mother rolled into one.

I waited till he left for a few days over Christmas and I moved into his apartment. I knew where he hid the key.

I unpacked and put everything away, leaving no hint of my recent arrival. I scrupulously created the impression of disorder among my things and mingled a few of them in with his, I divided the walk-in closet in two, I mixed our books together. I filled the fridge. I carefully scattered my toiletries around the bathroom, adding some dirty laundry too. I was cooking when he came in. In response to his alarm, I asked if he wasn't feeling well, if he wanted me to call a doctor. When he asked who I was, I acted surprised, indignant, laughing it off; I reminded him teasingly of our life together, ten years of it so far, mixing some of his memories into mine. I reeled off a list of our habits and then I went from laughter to tears. I cried a lot, I begged him to stop it, this act, it wasn't funny anymore. I asked him to call the friends we had in common, with whom I'd rehearsed the whole scene several times, and they played it to perfection. They keep our secret even now. That was two years ago. Out of pure luck—and for old personal reasons that I discovered almost by chance—he had always refused to discuss his previous partners with his parents: he could check nothing with them. I knew he had no contact with his neighbors. He consulted several memory specialists, none of whom could ever diagnose the pathology behind his partial amnesia. I know that one day something will betray me, but in the meantime I am here. He sees me, he looks at me, he touches me, and he's getting used to me.

✳

I heard him start the engine and, when I went outside, the dust from the path raised by his car was still hanging in the air. It stung my eyes, that's what made me cry.

＊

I can't stand it anymore, this being dragged awake at night that he puts me through, when I've fallen into a deep sleep and he comes to bed after me, loud and lumbering, not bothering to check if I'm already asleep.

＊

I had chapped fingers from the terrible cold, bandages on almost every joint. I wanted to write to him in spite of everything, so he would come back. Because my skin was so dry and damaged, I wrote in a funny way, without using my index finger, which was the worst affected. Curiously, my handicapped writing became more precise. I was forced to make an effort. Even my language was transformed by it, clarified. I was going to be able to tell him, to explain everything. I was going to be so clear that he would end up coming back. I made piles of rough drafts, for days and days, then, satisfied at last, when I set to copying them out, my index finger had healed. I had lost my precision, my clarity, my certainties.

＊

I love his cock. The most moving thing about the cock of the man I love is when it's soft, during trivial, everyday activities, in the shower or when he's asleep.

＊

All these moments when I'm alone but walking toward her, all these mornings when I'll be with her in a few kilometers, a few hours.

＊

He's sitting opposite me on the streetcar. Headphones on head, he is drawing. He has several colored pencils held in one hand, bunched together. Deaf to the world but not blind, he seems to be drawing a portrait of the little girl standing beside me. She has a very beautiful face stained by a birthmark, a band of pigmentation beneath the eyes that covers her cheeks almost completely. This burgundy band on her very pale skin looks like the inkblots that analysts make people interpret, or a carnival mask that has dropped down over her cheekbones. She seems ill at ease; she must get a lot of teasing at school. He smiles at me as if I were complicit in his drawing, a theft of ill favor. We must be the only ones to find her so beautiful. When the little girl gets off, I go up to him and take the liberty, since he smiled at me, of having a look at his sketchpad. He has drawn not the girl's face but mine, my ordinary face.

＊

He had a serene way of being in silent moments. I was never afraid of having nothing to say with him.

＊

Before coming home from work, she washes and changes in the workshop changing room. She takes off her green overalls, runs a towel over her face, washes her hands and forearms, and brushes her hair. Still she brings the scents of timber home with her and sometimes, stranded behind one ear, a shaving of alder, oak, beech, or silver birch. But it's in her mouth more than anywhere that I taste these different trees, because when the scents, colors, and grains can't help her, she has picked up the odd habit of chewing on the wood in order to identify it.

＊

I met him from behind. He was crouched down, facing the ground, tying his shoe. He was blocking traffic along the sidewalk, which was busy at that time of day. People stopped or simply slowed down, then moved apart, like a fabric drawn open by a zip, like flowing water parted by a rock in midstream.

✸

He wanted to change me, to make me more feminine. He would take me shopping, to the hairdresser, to the beautician. He wasn't tyrannical, the opposite really. He was always very sweet about it, but I was defenseless against his attentions. I felt gauche, ugly, humiliated.

✸

If all the men I've loved were able to cross-check the facts, if they knew each other, say, and if they were to get together and discuss me, they'd be scared stiff. I hope they never meet.

✸

I wasn't allowed to touch him, his body was off-limits. He was my first cousin and I was very young. He didn't want trouble but he found it hard to resist me. Sitting on the shore of the lake where we spent our vacations, he would bend over, head down between the arches of his folded legs, and offer me his back so I could draw on it with twigs: children's games, faint scratches that he then asked me to photograph for posterity. He had a lot of acne and I was allowed—privileged—to squeeze his zits. It was a gesture of extraordinary familiarity, such as I've never had with anyone else. We both knew you shouldn't do it, that it makes them worse, that the spots get bigger and spread, and that our parents might find us and not understand, but we couldn't stop ourselves. A few weeks before the summer, he would secretly stop taking his antibiotics for me. His back would be covered in blemishes: cuts from branches, red marks, and squeezed pimples. It wasn't serious; it would clear up in the autumn. We didn't know that soon he would be too old to come on family vacations.

※

Life with him is so easy and sweet and joyful. I have a feeling he's cheating.

※

He was a bit crazy at the time. He had begun a phase of experiments. One week was spent not talking while forcing himself to keep doing things such as going out to buy bread or going to the post office. Another week he did not seeing, with bandages over his eyes. There was a week of not hearing, with earplugs in his ears, a week of not going outside, and I forget what else. That particular day happened to be one in the week of not seeing. He was behind me in line at the bakery and I felt his hands land gently on my shoulders. I didn't know he was trying to find his way, I thought he was secretly feeling me up, at the very least he was stroking me. I turned around. He was blindfolded. At first I thought he was genuinely injured, but he leaned toward the source of my voice, worked his way around to my ear and, whispering, he set me straight. It was the very beginning of the week of not seeing and I wasn't allowed to help him out. We fell in love right away, and bumped into each other a lot. On the Sunday when I took off his blindfold and bandages, he said he still liked me. I was glad that the week of not talking was already over.

✳

I let him wash my hair in the sink. He meant it to be affectionate but I knew he found the little mounds of grease that formed tiny bumps on my head disgusting. He had a sweet name for them, though: cherries.

✳

He walked out on me so brutally that he left all his things behind. Perhaps he did it on purpose so he could go on haunting the house, pursuing me, stopping me from rebuilding my life. I put everything that could be given away into cardboard boxes for thrift shops. Sorting and putting away and boxing things up kept me busy; keeping busy held my pain at bay. I threw out whatever seemed too cumbersome or unusable. Soon there was nothing left except for his scarves. He had about twenty scarves, for all seasons. I think that's a lot of scarves, yet I can't bring myself to give them all up. I wear them. My daughter gets angry, she says that man still has me under his thumb, and what with me wrapping these things around my neck, he even has me on a leash. I don't know, it's just I'd rather not let them go to waste, they're lovely, expensive scarves. And yet, when I left the first one behind in the waiting room at the doctor's, I decided that I had other scarves, and I didn't go back to see if anyone had kept it for me. When the second one came off in the street I was in a hurry and didn't pick it up. I don't remember what I did with the third one, the mid-season one, which I wanted to put on yesterday, against the cold snap. This evening, I'd have liked to have the one that went so well with my blue dress but I can't find it anymore. I wonder if I've perhaps lent it to someone, but who?

✳

She wasn't there anymore. I was hardly sleeping, and eating very little, so little I stopped going to the bathroom.

My basic functions were abandoning me, just as she had; I didn't have the strength to cry, or even enough water in me for tears. When tears, hunger, thirst, and digestion returned, I realized that I was alive and that living, filling my belly, getting things moving, getting dirty, would help me to forget her.

✳

With him I always felt pleasure without showing it. I wouldn't fake it—on the contrary—I'd hide my orgasms from him.

✳

On the website of the secondary school where he teaches, the schedules for each class are available online. He teaches twelve or thirteen classes and I know he's part-time; at an hour per class, that's about a third of the students at the school. I can't see his schedule without the password. I need to see it. Since we split up, I miss him so much that knowing whether he's teaching or not will help me, I think, to bear his absence. Not just knowing when he's teaching but which class, which grade. Without his password I can't see his schedule, but I can pull up the schedule of each of the classes, one after the other. So I click on each class, one by one, eight groups of ninth graders, seven groups of eighth graders, eight groups of seventh graders, and eight groups of sixth graders. Thirty-one classes. I check if the students of class x, then those of class y, have Mr. D for art, and I note down the time and the day if they do. I meticulously recreate his schedule on an A3 sheet. I make a point of using a ruler for my straight lines and a different color for each grade level. When I've finished, I pin it up on the wall above my desk. I sit working and, from time to time, I look up, to find out where he's gone to. Now he's finished with the seventh graders, he has a break. He'll be grading some homework, or perhaps he's gone for a cigarette, he'll be chatting with colleagues, maybe nursing a cup of coffee in the staff room. On days he doesn't teach, outside the columns in my chart, it's a blank, I have no idea. I would like to be able to fill in the blank: meals, movies, walks, shopping, reading. I would use different colors, one for each activity, if I could write all the other activities in his week into my chart, and the great mystery of the school holidays. I'd work really hard at it. I'd make maps and trace his movements on them. I'd create an atlas of his daily life, compose an almanac just for him, with all the days of the year, all the hours, and all the minutes.

✳

Of the men I have loved, there are those who have helped me to write, who supported my work simply by their presence. And then there are those who would dismantle my book, methodically, jealously, with carefully chosen remarks, and upon any pretext at all, sentence by sentence.

✳

Everyone was going there, downstairs. I didn't have a girlfriend and I felt like it, that's all. She was known in the building, the girl on the ground floor. I may well have been the only one not to have tried it with her. So I did like all the other guys in the building: I downed a stiff drink to get over my nerves and I went down and rang her doorbell. It was a bit of a letdown, a rush job really, and I ran out of small talk afterward, while I was getting my clothes back on. I gave her a quick peck on the cheek and said Thank you, and then, damn it, it all went horribly wrong, she went and fell for me. She hung on to me, physically, desperately, and she was crying and asking me to stay. She told me I was the only one who'd kissed her, she knew I was in love with her, she'd been waiting for me forever. She clung with such determination that it started to hurt and I had to force her fingers open. She fell back onto the bed with her full weight.

✳

It was as if the world had faded. I'd just put my contacts in, so I took them out and put them back again. It was no good.

Everything was still beyond me, even if I squinted. Things were slipping away. It was as though reality was weeping, or perhaps that was me, but something between me and the world, some kind of water, an interference, was stopping me from seeing clearly. I thought my contacts must be dirty, so I cleaned them, put them in a third time, and yet again the world misted over. And then I heard him get up, this man I'd only just met, and I remembered that he wore contacts, too. I had put on his vision, and it didn't match my own.

✳

I loved my old aunt. I wanted to introduce her to him, or him to her, I didn't quite know which. We were to come by and take her for a walk. We parked and he got out to help her. He helped my aunt climb into the car, as if it were nothing. I could have married him then and there.

✳

There's nothing between us anymore. I'm waiting. While I wait, I'm making an inventory. I wonder if there's much of us in the store of days to come.

✳

When I'm with him, I laugh so much that it hurts next to my ears, by my temples, where my jaw begins. It feels as though it's too tight there, at the endpoint of my laugh. I'd like to loosen this spot up now, to say stop it, as though I could just detach whatever's pulling at my face, as if it were as simple as letting some hair out of a hair clip. I'd like to undo whatever it is about being happy that tenses and tightens your whole skin. He's the one who got us all trussed up, he's the one who tied me in knots of laughter.

✳

No one sees what I see when I look at her.

✳

I was at something of a loss in those parts, knowing no one. Despite the boundless light of the gulf and the mildness of the cold season, I missed my family, my friends, and my hometown. I was out driving aimlessly, one bored, homesick Sunday. It was already dark. Suddenly, it began to rain very heavily. I saw someone walk into my headlights. Soaked through, the man looked like a bum, and I thought no one would ever pick him up. I stopped, although I would never normally pick up hitchhikers. He said I was a lifesaver. He had broken down and left his phone at home, and had been on his feet for hours now. If I would be so kind as to take him back home, he would reimburse me. He wasn't homeless; he had a luxurious villa on the coast. He insisted on offering me a glass of wine in his palace.

＊

He is fascinated by bridges and aqueducts, of all dimensions and every material, from tiny wooden bridges to monumental viaducts; anything that spans a gap or a waterway. We spend all our free time hunting them down. He marks their positions by covering our maps with crosses, which we drive between, linking them up like children playing connect the dots.

＊

When he's getting dressed, his arms become fins.

＊

She gets up before me every day. I don't hear her, I hardly even feel her getting out of bed. Still half-asleep, I sense her moving around the apartment, very far away at first, but then, little by little, her movements, her soft morning noises, grow closer and closer, and, slowly, gently, one layer of awareness after another, I wake up.

✳

My memory of him is the stretched skin of a drum. At the slightest touch, it vibrates and resounds.

✳

He comes to see me, closes the shutters, and takes me in his arms. Darkness falls at midday for us alone: not the darkness of deep ocean shades but a pastel darkness, where the colors mistake the time and hesitate to be what they are.

✳

She likes order and cleanliness. Everything in our home is neat and tidy. But she sheds her hair, constantly. And, I have no idea how come, she still has plenty of hair on her head, as much as ever, perhaps even more. The more of her hairs I find on the floor, the wilder her mop grows. She grumbles as she picks them up. I enjoy tracking them down, little refugees evading her vigilance.

*

After she left, her smell stayed for a few days, especially in the bedroom. Now it has become so faint that I'm surely just imagining it. I tried to preserve it by sleeping on the living-room sofa. I didn't change the sheets in the bedroom, didn't air it out, but what with my coming and going, trying to capture traces of her, I must have driven out her smell. Tonight I'll sleep in the bed again. My back hurts; I hurt all over. I can't fight her disappearance any longer. She'll be there under the covers when I slide in, I'll breathe her in one last time, and tomorrow I'll change the sheets and throw the window wide open.

*

We were cold in the forest and the fog made us huddle close to each other. We were caught up in our own rustlings, the moist air holding every noise close to us. This cocoon of sound kept us in whispers, as though we were lovers.

*

When I look at all these cushions finely embroidered for me by my husband during his long months at sea, I can't imagine him delicately handling the fabric in the evenings, after the brutality of a day's fishing, the violence of the swell, the chapped skin, the punch of each squall. I can't imagine his hands becalmed at their work, and yet.

✳

I only found out he was dead weeks after he disappeared. I had looked everywhere and called him endlessly. I thought he was playing dead because of our endless, increasingly unbearable fights. I knew he was still in love with her. She was his last and only love—I'd heard him say those very words to her on the phone, and I'd been hurt, terribly hurt. That was the main subject of our arguments, really. Yet we'd been together, he and I, for years, and he called every evening and panicked if I wasn't home. We weren't living together; he didn't want to, because of her. I was the one who comforted him, who listened, I was there for him. I consoled him. I didn't know that she alone appeared in his day planner under the line "In the event of an emergency, please contact…" But she didn't get there in time when they called her, all wrapped up as she was in her new life, her new love. She had moved on long ago. She was away, and as they weren't together now, she and he, and as they weren't that close anymore either, she didn't give him her number when she went away for the weekend on a family vacation. I still did, because he asked me to, because he wanted to know where I was. He wanted to be able to call me at the drop of a hat.

He didn't want to go on vacation with me, he didn't want to dishonor her memory by traveling with me. I used to go away by myself but he knew how to reach me, always. He died alone. I found out from her, when I made up my mind to call him at her house, thinking, maybe, just maybe. She told me she had gotten the message from the hospital too late. She was on vacation, and in any case she couldn't have gone and held him in his last moments, it wasn't her place. She said I have my life you see, and I thought you were with him, I thought you'd been informed, although, that said, I couldn't understand why you weren't at the funeral.

✳

She has fallen asleep with the notes from her medical course still in her hands. I come into the bedroom, bend over her, and lift the pages away one by one so as not to wake her. Then I pull the sheet up to her shoulders, stand up, and turn out the light.

✳

Her voice modulates with her emotions, as if, inside her, life were turning dials on a mixing table, or as if her throat harbored an erratic performer messing with the tuning of her vocal cords. Sometimes the hopeless musician is me. I can't take these changes of frequency, particularly when her emotional voice goes sharp and saturated. Particularly when I'm to blame. But I think I love her for her voice, even so, for this betrayal of her emotions via her mouth. For this transparency. Only joy can draw harmonious cadences from that voice, which it makes strangely deep and low. She stays silent when she knows that she's vulnerable, but she doesn't always know when that is.

✳

I was off guard, had forgotten the scorches, signs of the concealed fire that goes on consuming trees from below. Underground incubation. Above ground it seemed to have gone out. I should have guessed that it might revive, creeping up along the roots, in another place and at another time, perhaps even in the heart of winter. The holes dug by foraging animals drew it like chimneys. One tree ringed with snow, suddenly and all by itself, caught fire. I could have paid more attention to the steam rising from the ground, but really all appeared quiet and the winter landscape was so familiar. And the fire that I had thought quite out, that memory of her, flared again.

✳

The old floorboards have come loose and bits of dirt get caught between the planks. I try to suck them out with the vacuum cleaner nozzle. It was during one of these wearying attempts at housework that I found the delicate gold bracelet, which he had given me and I had lost right away, scarcely worn. The vacuum cleaner swallowed it, and it made a tinny jingling that was overpowered by the great roar of suction. It was hardly audible. Hardly, but I heard it, like a droning background noise, like a worry. I turned the vacuum cleaner off and opened the dust filter—it's a bagless machine. I saw something gleaming in the gray wad that was making me cough. That something is in my pocket now. I don't dare put it back on my wrist, for fear of losing it again, as I lost him.

✳

She doesn't like me to join her in the garden; for her, it's an intimate place. She believes you can see a woman's passion in her garden. I don't ask her anymore, and she brings me enormous flowers.

✳

To live amid beauty was fundamental for him. I didn't understand. I thought that beauty was something separate, that you couldn't live inside it, only look at it from afar, from the outside, and only very rarely touch it. Or I thought it could be inside us, well hidden, shielded. It was not a stage set, a mere appearance. But he refused to make a rare event of it or a secret; it was his minimum requirement. Our bodies, our house, our things, everything had to be beautiful. Otherwise, he would say, we can't go on. He found me fat, dowdy, and brash, brash in how I dressed and the way I spoke. I was ugly and gauche. Because I loved him, I lost fifteen kilos, let him choose my clothes, and above all, I took to living in silence, afraid that with my noise, my everyday noise, the noise of my life, I would annoy him. He thought I was vulgar in spite of everything. I would have liked to shout, to really test the limits of our bodies and our voices; I would have liked to shout, play, take pleasure. I thought that's what living was about.

✹

He is lying on his back with his right arm up, thrown back, forearm under his head. I settle into the inviting hollow, with my ear up against his armpit. The pulse beating there drums into me. It breathes, more a labor of the lungs than of the heart, like the weariness of a wave as it reaches the pebbles.

✹

In that hotel the lighting in the corridors is automatic. We had it out with each other there right through till dawn, whispering so as not to wake the other guests. The movements of our bodies were picked up by the lasers and kept setting off the lights. Our gestures were violent, muffled and violent. He wouldn't let me back into the room, he was gripping me by the arm, sometimes he tried to kiss me—one last time, he said—sometimes I felt sure he was going to hit me, and all this, this moving around, the last agonies of our love, under the constant on-and-off of the lights. We were breaking up in darkness and in blazing light, my tears by turns extinguished and illuminated. We said a coruscating goodbye.

✳

She prefers winter for the clothes, for the feeling of having to cover your body. It makes her feel alive, desirable even. And it's true: she is more beautiful in winter. She says that dressing yourself is a very organic act: you feel a bit chilly and want to protect your body, you want to snuggle, to hunker down. She shuns the summer, when everyone is half-naked and there's no mystery left. Come winter, she envelops herself in several layers of clothing. She shivers and glows.

✳

I thought I would never recover from our breakup, but life—or whatever it is, I believe it's called life—I didn't want to let life go. One morning I woke up not so sad and I felt ready, even eager, to look at myself in the mirror. I knew I had aged suddenly; I had felt it. I had wept so much over those last few weeks, I wasn't surprised by the shadows under my eyes. I saw a hair gleam, I'd been expecting that, too. I took a pair of tweezers to try to seize it and pluck it out. I wasn't thirty yet, it was too soon. I didn't want this, not yet, but it hid, then gleamed again, and got away. Finally I succeeded in pulling it out, and the shaft wasn't white but golden. I examined the hair up close, held it in the light. Yes, golden. I looked back at myself in the mirror and saw others, glinting here and there. I'd gone gold.

✳

I found out that he was writing down everything about us, and storing our outings, our presents, and journeys, not in a diary but in the form of archives, with tickets and boarding passes as evidence. His cellar was lined with shelves stuffed with files, all categorized by periods of time and by names. Girls' names. Mine only took up half a shelf.

✳

He suffers from persistent, all-encompassing impatience, with people, with life's milestones, with the weather forecast, with trivialities. All these big and little things that end up happening, always happen too late for him. And with me: he's impatient with me too. He tells me I dither, that I'm delaying, he hurries me just as he hurries everything around him.

❋

I had put a lot of thought into how best to transport the flowers, early daffodils that I'd picked that very morning. I wanted to bring him a little piece of my life, a sample of the spring. I loved him, and he really loved flowers. He lived in the city. We weren't getting along so well anymore and I wanted to show him I still believed in us. I had wrapped the daffodils carefully in a wet cotton napkin, which I folded around them to make a protective cone. I'd tied my bouquet with string and was holding it upside down. I held it like that, upside down, the whole way, never once putting it down, even in the bus and on the train, for fear of crushing the flowers. I had only one hand free to deal with everything else, my suitcase, my bag, my jacket, my sandwich. The daffodils poked the triangular tips of their petals, little golden tongues, through the opening in the napkin cone, which was at the bottom, as I was holding the bunch the wrong way up. I was taking such care with my movements that it felt as if I were handling a flaming torch, illuminating the aisle of the bus from floor level. But I was worried not that it might flare up but that it might die out, that the yellow wouldn't last. I kept peeking inside the napkin to check how the flowers were doing, and I watered them carefully out of the cap of my water bottle. Everything was going okay, they were holding out. He was waiting for me on the platform. He said Are they for me? It wasn't really a question. He looked happy, and he thanked me and took the bunch. When we got to his house, he put the daffodils in a vase while I unpacked my suitcase. In only a few minutes they had wilted.

＊

After his accident, my husband wasn't my husband anymore. He was in an irreversible coma. I went to see him every day and stayed a long while, talking to him, trying in vain to get him back. I would read books to him. One morning I had no more words, no more books, and no more courage but I still went to see him, mute and empty-handed. I took off my scarf because it was so warm. I felt stifled in that hospital. Without thinking, I ran the scarf between his fingers very gently, stroking his hand with the fabric. He caught hold of it.

＊

I wonder if, when they hear the banging that seems to be coming from our apartment, our neighbors think he's doing some renovations, even late at night, or if they hear me too, whimpering and begging him to stop.

✳

It was very cold. I hadn't put gloves on. I defrosted my fingers between my thighs before letting them touch his skin.

✳

Everyone knows he has a mistress, but it doesn't occur to anyone that it might be me. A friend even said to me, before backpedaling clumsily At least with your body you're beyond suspicion, sorry, but well, you know what I mean, don't take it the wrong way. I am unthinkable; no, it couldn't possibly be me. I wonder if he only keeps me secret out of fear of his wife's reaction or if he, too, is ashamed of my unfortunate appearance.

✳

We've been together for so long, she and I, we're so close, that with time and growing intimacy, our periods have become synchronized.

✳

He left me for something blonde and beautiful. Something he couldn't do without, so he said. Not without those colors, that sandy hue, the yellow and ocher limestone bronzed by the glow of distant Spanish sunshine, that whiff of the sea in the salt-thick air of high tide, those gilded waters, the pale, diamond-shaped paving stones, the rows of little stalls that let the whole sky into the streets, and the scent of pine trees. He said Just imagine having the greatest forest in Europe at your feet, and as if that weren't enough, trees on every corner. He told me of soaring bamboo fronds emerging from invisible gardens, of mimosas, acacias in bloom, villas draped with oleanders, and cherry trees bringing a touch of Japan to the wide boulevards. He wanted to see the boats again. He wanted to plunge once more into that multimillionaire history, those ancient memories that seep from every wall, the memories of all the men and all the women who live, eat, sleep, play, love, suffer, shout, weep, and laugh there. I was jealous of that town, and I had every reason to be.

✳

We are getting old. I like the signs of aging on him, the wrinkles and folds, the emergence of moles and liver spots. I wonder if these marks appear all of a sudden or little by little. I look out for the signs of these blossomings. Time is pollinating his skin with flowers, with speckles, with stars.

✳

We're the same shape: same profile, same outline. I can hide behind her, she behind me. In the sun, our shadows attach to the wrong bodies.

✳

My wife is a pianist. Her fingers can master Monk and Albéniz, Mehldau and Scriabin, anybody.

✳

I can't live fully. I'm not really there, even when I'm with her. I'm dormant. When she drags me toward life I feel coerced, like an animal woken from hibernation too early by some error in its internal clock or an abrupt and unexpected change of temperature. This disturbance, this change that I feel, is her. She's too surprising, too alive, too springlike; I'm not ready.

※

In the shower, the falling water redraws the shape of her spine.

※

All the witnesses to our wedding are gone. We had two each, four friends. His are dead, one from cancer, the other from a heart attack. One of mine fell out with us so badly that we don't dare contact her again, and no one has heard from the other one for ages, not even her own husband or her grown-up children. She walked out one day, leaving a letter saying she didn't want anyone to go looking for her. He and I started to grow apart around the time we lost the first one. After his friend's death, he resented me for not having been welcoming enough when he used to come and see us, before it was too late. From then on, we couldn't stop feeling angry with each other about trifles, about the children we hadn't had, about everything and nothing. By the time we lost the last one, we had already embarked on the long, grueling process of divorce. Now we've no witnesses left. Who is there to say that we were once in love?

＊

Sometimes I want her so much that my legs wobble. As though I were a newborn deer trying to stand up.

＊

He's got a few very long whiskers growing around his nose that stand up straight, like antennae. A gigantic insect smiling at me. It's quite astonishing. I wonder why he doesn't pluck them out. As if he has read my mind, he says that there are no differences between people and no handicaps, only variants. These outsize, erectile whiskers are his variant, his version, tickling me whenever I touch them.

＊

I met him when I called a wrong number. His voice was so lovely, saying I must have made a mistake, that I couldn't bring myself to hang up.

＊

We were each convinced that we'd found traces of the other. We knew he was cheating on us; we didn't know each other but we both, separately, knew that the other existed, despite his denials and his precautions. Sometimes we wondered if there wasn't a third woman, but we were never sure. About the two of us, though, there was no doubt. He had bought us a little toiletry set, just one, telling each of us, of course, that it was for her alone, a set to keep at his place. He wanted to make sure neither of us left something in the bathroom for the other one to find. He had picked two women with the same hair color. I'm not sure he did it on purpose, because he did clearly prefer brunettes, but it suited him given all the hairs left behind on the sofa, on the shoulder of his sweater, all over the place. We were about the same height, so we came up to the same place when we hugged him. He gave us the same perfume. When I pulled her hairs out of the brush, he would smile and say, you see, they're brown. Brown they may have been, but they weren't mine. They were ever-so-slightly wavier, these hairs, and I had dandruff. I pictured her finding it on our shared hairbrush. And being shocked, denying she had it.

✳

Between us, nothing is dirty. After exploring inside me with all of his fingers, he cleans his hand, licking it slowly.

✳

He sprays a mist of water onto his newspaper to stop the pages from rustling as he reads next to me while I sleep.

✳

I wait for him. I divide the time into small sections and try to busy myself, filling the time as if it were space. I divide it up, breaking it down into little units like at school, years ago, when I was so bored that I used to draw and then color in fifty-five boxes to make an hour-long lesson go by more quickly. I concoct lots of little strategies to keep me going until the day he gets back. I invent things to do to color in my latest set of boxes. My life is built around a countdown. My heart has become a clock, an hourglass, a very precise timer that I want to set to the day, the hour, and the minute of his flight home. But he still hasn't told me when he's coming back.

✳

He wasn't very good at using his cell phone. He left me messages by accident, which were usually just the sound of him walking. I listened to them right to the end.

＊

I don't know if they'll find the letters and photos, all the little presents, the humble keepsakes of our love. I'm not quite all there anymore, as they say. I'm well aware of that, and I didn't protest about the retirement home, only I'm worried about what will happen to my little hoard. I'd like to take them with me, all these secret things to do with her. But how? I'm watching my children moving my things, shifting the furniture. I wanted to be here while they sort everything out. I'm in my corner, not bothering them. They're so kind, so thoughtful, and supportive. They're trying to spare me any trouble. I'm afraid they'll find my treasure trove, and afraid they won't find it, that I won't be able to take it with me. I've hardly anything left here of their mother; they divided everything between them when she died. But then there's her, this other woman, whose existence they don't even suspect, and there are so many mementos of her that I'd like to keep. How can I do it without them knowing?

＊

I stroke the earplugs he left on my bedside table. The wax has molded itself to the hollows of his ears. I take them in my palm, keeping the imprint of that fragile place warm. I am holding his hearing; I have his sleep in my hand.

＊

For our training sessions, we only had one big towel between the two of us. Instead of using it one after the other, we used it together, each holding one end. We met up in the middle.

＊

I get a funny feeling when I say his name in public and he's not there. The first and last name of the man I love. I do it all the time.

＊

As I slip my cock between her breasts, I try to feel a heartbeat. I want her to push them tightly together, to close them around me, and at the same time I dream of her opening herself up, pulling her chest apart with both hands until she's unbuttoning her rib cage, until I can feel, beating next to my cock so tightly pressed against it, her naked heart.

＊

It was hot and we were on vacation, just he and I for once. We were eating ice cream at the outside tables. The strap of my little summer dress suddenly broke and I only just managed to hold it up in time. He said Don't move. He got up and I watched him make his way toward the hotel. He was back very soon with the sewing kit from the room, and, shifting his chair up to mine, he mended my strap, right there on me, patiently, skillfully. His movements were precise and delicate, and he took great care with the needle, snapping the thread with his teeth right next to my skin.

✳

By taking all these photos, he transforms the landscape where we walk. I sometimes wonder if he isn't really a photographer at all, but a magician instead.

✳

Other people's smells bother me, as they do everyone. But not hers, not her special smell, her intimate, bedroom smell, her smell mixed with mine. I love our smells of warm, rubbed skin, persistent as the scent of the almond blossom that she cut and then abandoned in a vase, our musty smells. It makes her feel queasy when we've made love a lot and the room starts to smell strongly. She throws the flowers away at the first sign of wilting. She airs the room, opening the windows wide.

✳

It's as though you had to know the password for our relationship.

✳

He was always criticizing my smile. I smiled a lot, it's true. I was happy to be with him. He said that because I smiled so often, I had a sort of silly-little-girl smirk permanently stuck on my face.

✳

In his closets, drawers, and cupboards he has so many clothes, shoes, pants, hats, and gloves, all in different cloths and materials, natural and artificial, wool, silk, linen, rayon, cotton, acrylic, leather, snakeskin, and vinyl, outfits in all sorts of styles, from the most vulgar to the most sophisticated, from the ordinary to the wild, for all ages and even in different sizes, for all parts of his body, from his head to his feet, legs, knees, thighs, hips, stomach, shoulders, neck, arms, and hands, that I suspect him of being several men, of being all men in one.

✳

We engraved our love onto the tree, inscribing the bark with hearts pierced with arrows and our initials inside. It wasn't exactly original, but I'll always remember the bark's welcoming softness. He went off to a big city to study ethnology. I knew it was pointless waiting for him. He would meet girls who were more refined and cultivated but I'd still be a country girl and soon he'd be ashamed of me. He swore never to forget me, shedding great, fat tears that I didn't believe in for a second. That was fifteen years ago. Yesterday I got a piece of birch bark in the mail from Russia, along with a letter in handwriting that I knew right away was his. He wrote that there, this bark is symbolically associated with the blossoming of young women, and is therefore an appropriate material for love letters. And on the bark there's another letter for me.

✳

With her, I had that seesaw feeling of being almost happy, on the verge of a new beginning, and the certainty that always came too: this won't last.

*

When we're lying in bed, if he touches me and doesn't move away again, I instantly want to retreat, to turn over and change position. I can't stay there touching him. I get pins and needles, stiff legs, sometimes even cramps. It's almost painful. When we embrace and we keep moving, it's fine, but I can't stand sleeping in the fixed clinch of someone's arms. My body refuses and pulls away.

*

He isn't very relaxed in groups, and at the slightest hint of emotion, he stutters. He stutters saying my name, and I love it. I think he's noticed, so he does it a lot, calls out to me, says my name. When we're alone he never stutters, but as soon as we're out in public, having a drink with friends, he turns to me on the slightest pretext, multiplying my name in his mouth.

*

I'll never dare tell him how I feel. In my language we "confess" how we feel, as if to feel were a fault, an error of taste, a lack of tact, or perhaps a linguistic mistake. There's none of that between us. No linguistic mistakes, that's for sure. Besides, we see each other so rarely, we two, and even more rarely alone, "en tête-à-tête," as we say, that I don't know how I could even begin to talk to him. And yet I am "en tête-à-tête" with him almost constantly, when I'm working on his books. I'm in his head, in his language, in his sentences. One day I bumped into his wife, we even had a chat, and I realized that she doesn't know him as well as I do, I who spend my time probing his most intimate thoughts and examining his every word as I translate his books into French.

✳

As she left she told me her name and said See you soon. I didn't know anything else about her, just her first name. I had no way of contacting her. The memory of her face and her name stayed with me for days and days. I couldn't think about anything else, couldn't concentrate on other things, couldn't even look anywhere except within, at this memory, my ears ringing. I felt as if my head were underwater and it was she who was pulling me under, drowning me.

✳

I packed my bags again. I couldn't stand her ex-boyfriend. In a jealous rage he had broken into her apartment, to which he'd kept the keys, and had stolen all my papers: my passport, my ID card, everything. I'd been there moments before, to drop off a few boxes and bags at her place, and then I'd gone back to mine to pick up the rest. This time I was moving in. When I saw my things scattered around everywhere, I didn't realize at first that it was him. I went to the police station to report the theft. It took forever, and on the way back I saw myself, in close-up, plastered all over the neighborhood, in telephone booths, in store windows, on walls, windows, and telephone poles, my passport photo blown up on wanted posters, with a phone number underneath that wasn't mine or my girlfriend's. I called her and told her the number. She didn't seem surprised. She said That's his number, he'll never let me rebuild my life, he's crazy about me. She sounded almost reassured as she said it. She wasn't even angry.

✺

The colors filtering through the window were strangely vivid for that time of the morning. It looked more like midday, or even the afternoon. Opening my eyes, I felt that sense of urgency of being late, of having overslept. How long had it been light? I sat up abruptly, and she woke up and asked what time it was. I told her not to worry, to go back to sleep. I was relieved; it was still early. The sense of urgency was her: the intensity of the colors, the eddying of time, the tangled hours. There she was, sleeping beside me. It made everything a blur.

＊

He was the love of my commute. We loved each other for all those years on the streetcar going to and from work. Twenty minutes there, twenty minutes back, every working day of the year. We couldn't do very much, a few kisses, a few caresses, but we talked a lot and we knew each other's lives inside out, all our dreams and disappointments. We were both in relationships, and we exchanged news of our children, looked forward to being reunited after family vacations, and supported each other through hard times, all in twenty-minute slots.

＊

My husband chases storms in the middle of the night. Not quite like the man in the Brassens song, but almost. He doesn't install lightning conductors but he does set up a tripod for his camera. Equipped with the latest technology and receiving a constant stream of data, live radar maps, and weather updates via his cell, he waits for the sky to unroll its carnival. His heart beats faster as soon as the innocent, fair-weather clouds take on what he calls vertical extension. He says that each cloud is a bearer of aesthetic potential. He's always thinking several days ahead, poring over barometric readings, setting his compasses, and sweet-talking his sensors. He has always watched the skies: as a small boy he was already chasing the shadows of cumulus clouds, trying to work out their speed and altitude.

He covers insane distances, hundreds of kilometers for a few photos in the dark, even if he has work early the next day, even if I ask him to stay home. He jumps into his car and drives after the storm, following it wherever it goes. If something stops him, if he hits the shoreline, say, when the storm is developing out at sea, then the myth, the mystery, and the fear of it are amplifed still further. He loves inaccessible ocean thunderstorms. He doesn't like safe little urban ones. He seeks out storms in the middle of nowhere in untamed skies, aerial tidal waves that make him feel tiny. He describes cloud streets, strange cloud alignments sculpted by the flow of the wind at different altitudes, the special smell of the road when it starts to rain and the storm is poised to break, and eventually crackling sounds, the deep, cavernous voice of thunder, the reek of burning, blue halos and luminous branchings that fill the sky with dazzling foliage. He tells me there is often a period of calm before the end when you can't see anymore electrical activity and then, savagely, one vast flash voids the whole storm.

Once the storm has passed, all the energy amassed by the high pressure drops away, and then, only then, does he realize how far from home he is. He wonders how he's going to make it all the way back again. Lost and forlorn, he calls me.

✸

On the telephone my heart beats so hard that it feels like it's inside the handset. I can hear it thumping against the receiver. I so wanted him to call, and now his voice is distorted by the echoing in my chest.

✳

When I penetrate her I feel her organs and intestines, her muscles, tendons, and bones, as if they were live animals in a cage. That cage is me; she is enclosed by my skin wrapped around hers.

✳

He has become amnesiac after a bout of encephalitis. He can't make new memories. If he wants to remember something, he now has to do it with me. He hates being dependent, needing our life together in order to remember things. His memory is carried within our shared lives. Anything he does alone will be lost. He resents me, doesn't trust me, even though before his illness we already had a shared memory. But he's become suspicious, he suspects me of inventing some things and deleting others, of creating false memories for him. He uses a notebook to keep track. Sometimes he's the one who's actually inventing memories: he also suffers from what the doctors call confabulation, believing in memories that don't exist, mixing up times or places. Apparently this is common in amnesiacs. He's becoming paranoid. He thinks I write in his notebook, that I go through correcting it, so now he's training himself to recognize his own writing. He spends hours looking for signs of my hand, for clues pointing to my interference in his paper memories. For him, writing down each day's events and activities requires a lot of effort and concentration. He doesn't know how to choose, to choose without being able to wait and see what needs to be retained in order to remember. So he writes very quickly and messily. He can't read what he has written.

*

What I like best about our walks are the steep parts, when my body is too little, my reach too short, and I have to scramble and leap: he holds out his hand, opens his arms wide to catch me.

*

After showering, before going to bed, he always had a little damp patch on his underwear. I never knew, even after many years, if it was from going to the toilet, a stray droplet after peeing, or else arousal at the lovemaking to come. I never dared ask.

＊

He was taking a whole load of medication: tranquilizers, antidepressants, sleeping pills, the lot. I replaced them all with love notes. Little phrases, scribbled on scraps of paper. Hundreds, thousands of them. I found a website selling pharmaceutical products and ordered some little transparent capsules in packs of five hundred. I inserted my miniscule rolled-up writings into each capsule. To be read daily, morning, noon, and night.

＊

I couldn't stop thinking about him even while I was doing other things. At work, in bed, with the children, out walking, getting up in the morning, eating, going to bed, doing housework, reading, showering, doing nothing. In the end I managed to forget about him for a few moments by concentrating intently on my body in a yoga class. We did posture after posture, during which I no longer thought of him or myself or my suffering, during which all I thought about was my movements and my breathing. In a posture that I wasn't very good at, mid-twist and eyes closed, I managed to catch my hair, with my arms stretched out behind me, and then, suddenly, I felt him. I thought he was standing close, his hand on the back of my neck.

＊

It was enough for me to hear that soft throat-clearing, that sound belonging to him alone.

＊

She looked at me. We came to a halt, the world and I. All the machines were stilled, the wind was gagged, the leaves on the trees didn't dare a single flutter, and all the people and all the animals were quiet, frozen like musical statues, except for her. She continued to move and talk and smile at me, as if nothing had happened.

＊

He lived on the same street as me, directly opposite, but I never managed to make it over the crosswalk. I would take my baby in my arms and go and stand at the crossing every day. The cars sometimes stopped for me but I stayed on my side. Every day for years I went and stood at that crossing. There were more and more cars. Workmen came and installed a traffic light. My baby grew up and became a little boy who held my hand, and when he stood with me at the crossing he asked me why we didn't go over when the little man was green. Then he became a big boy who stopped asking questions and didn't come with me anymore. I never knew if he saw me, if he saw us, his son and me, if he saw us standing at the crossing.

✴

I realized that he had feelings for me, something akin to trust, when I noticed that he was only speaking to me.

✴

I celebrated Three Kings' Day with my lover, my sister, and my childhood friend, the three women in my life. We were invited to my sister's house; her husband and their children were also there, and my best friend's partner. It was he who cut the king cake and passed around the slices according to the confused orders of the kids under the table. With the first bite, I felt the little figurine in my mouth. I was just about to claim the crown when I remembered that I would have to choose my queen. Of the three women in my life, how could I choose my queen for a day? I looked at them each in turn and then, discreetly, I swallowed the figurine.

✴

My native tongue is sign language. My parents were deaf but I'm not. When they died, much too young, I had no one to speak our language with and I could no longer share what I was feeling. It's not the same in spoken or written French. I miss my language, the language in which my parents explained the world to me, my language of discovery. I fell in love with her when I realized that she hadn't heard me come up behind her. She gave a start and smiled, and right away I signed Hello, to which she responded shyly. I thought that through her I would rediscover everything. But she has worked and struggled for years to learn to speak just like everyone else, to forget sign language, the sign of her handicap. She won't speak it anymore.

✳

I didn't know she was there. She had curled up and gone to sleep in my armchair.

✳

I went out, turned right down my street, and that's when I saw her. Or rather, not her really, not yet. First I saw the marks of high heels in the snow—ridiculous—then a little farther on, marks where they had slipped—what a surprise—then some churned-up snow, and just after that a crater shape on the ground, followed by more stiletto marks, very neat prints, as if nothing had happened. I looked up. The woman teetering ahead of me, head held high, was soaking wet all down the back of her coat. I caught up with her and asked if she'd hurt herself, and if she'd like to take my arm.

✳

I was a railroad-crossing guard, like my parents. I was born in this little house on the edge of the tracks, amid the rumble and reassuring punctuality of the trains, and when my parents retired I took up their duties. They moved out. I was almost thirty and I couldn't leave the house, couldn't leave the railroad crossing. I didn't know anybody and didn't know anything about life. He got me out of there. I believed in his nonsense, his easy calm. I thought I was free in my brand-new, silent house but I missed the roar of the trains and he was always out, only ever passing through, like the trains used to, but silently and irregularly. After a while you get used to the trains, you don't see them anymore, or even hear them. You know the timetables by heart, you time your life by them. But I couldn't get used to him. I would wait up for him to come home, never knowing when he'd be back. There was no point in waking up at certain times to open the gate ahead of him, in the same way I always used to get up and go and put the barrier down.

After our divorce, I was able to return to my parents'

house; the railway company had put it up for sale for a negligible sum because of the noise pollution. I hear the signal announcing that the barriers are closing but I don't move, then I hear the familiar boom of the train. Everything's automatic now. There's no more railroad-crossing guard. I'm safe inside my house, my time marked out by the regular vibrations. The barrier keeps me safe.

※

Her body is so supple she could be made of cloth, long bandages rolled around each other, a bundle of elastic flesh that she unwinds when she wraps herself around me.

※

He sits down cross-legged on the pebbly riverbank and takes a drawing pad and pencil case from his backpack. I sit near him, not too near, with a book and a hat. He gives me a smile and sets to work. He might be drawing a deer. Or a tree, perhaps. I resist the urge to ask questions or go over and look. His arms make branching movements but I don't know if his charcoal is creating the antlers of a deer or the arms of a tree. Soon there are new shoots appearing with every gesture of his hands, and his fingertips sprout twigs. Birds come and perch. I don't know where all these birds come from; robins, sparrows, blue tits, chaffinches, even magpies, swallows, and gulls, birds of the vine and the meadow, birds of the lakes and the streams, birds of the mountains and the sea, birds of the forests and the glades, birds from far-off places, hummingbirds. There they are beside him, wings folded, some so tiny that they stand on a single pebble. And then, from pebble to pebble, they hop right up to him, from pebble to pebble, not flying, they come closer, climb his calves, scale his legs, and hop onto his knees, explore his thighs, his wrists, his arms, settle on his shoulders and his bare head, look at his sketches. And sing.